"You don't have to w
door, Jack. I'm a big

He nodded.

But he waited all the same.

Chloe knew he wouldn't drive away just because she'd told him to. He'd wait until she got inside. She supposed it should irritate or frustrate her, but considering her parents hadn't cared that much about her when she'd been a *child*, she couldn't muster up taking offense to Jack's tendency to overprotect.

Hell, she didn't just not take offense—she downright loved it. She'd been taking care of herself and everyone else her whole life. She'd even dedicated her life to a job that protected other people, best she could.

Yeah, she didn't mind someone out there caring enough to protect *her* for once.

And that is why you find yourself in a dysfunctional, secret relationship.

COLD CASE DISCOVERY

NICOLE HELM

Harlequin
INTRIGUE

For anyone who has made something good
in the midst of tragedy.

ISBN-13: 978-1-335-45715-8

Recycling programs
for this product may
not exist in your area.

Cold Case Discovery

Copyright © 2025 by Nicole Helm

For questions and comments about the quality of this book, please contact us at
CustomerService@Harlequin.com.

TM and ® are trademarks of Harlequin Enterprises ULC.

Harlequin Enterprises ULC
22 Adelaide St. West, 41st Floor
Toronto, Ontario M5H 4E3, Canada
www.Harlequin.com

Printed in U.S.A.

Nicole Helm grew up with her nose in a book and the dream of one day becoming a writer. Luckily, after a few failed career choices, she gets to follow that dream—writing down-to-earth contemporary romance and romantic suspense. From farmers to cowboys, Midwest to *the* West, Nicole writes stories about people finding themselves and finding love in the process. She lives in Missouri with her husband and two sons, and dreams of someday owning a barn.

CAST OF CHARACTERS

Jack Hudson—Oldest Hudson sibling, sheriff of Sunrise and leader of Hudson Sibling Solutions.

Chloe Brink—Sheriff's deputy of Sunrise.

Ry Brink—Chloe's brother.

Mary & Walker Daniels—Jack's sister, who handles admin at HSS, and her husband, who also works for HSS.

Cash & Izzy Hudson—Jack's brother and niece. Cash trains dogs for a living.

Carlyle Daniels—Walker's sister, who is dating Cash.

Zeke Daniels—Walker's brother.

Anna, Hawk & Caroline Steele—Jack's youngest sister, who also works for HSS, her husband, who is a fire investigator, and their baby.

Grant & Dahlia Hudson—Jack's brother and his wife. Grant works for HSS, and Dahlia is a librarian.

Palmer & Louisa Hudson—Jack's brother and his wife. Palmer works for HSS, and Louisa works at her parents' orchard.

Chapter One

Her phone trilled in the dark.

Chloe Brink rolled over to find the other side of the bed empty, which was good. *Best*. Considering the screen on her phone read *Do Not Answer*.

In other words, it wasn't work or something important. It was her brother calling her. At two in the morning.

She loved her baby brother and wished she could save him, but he was an addict. And until he accepted that, until *he* decided he wanted to change, her relationship with him had to be distant.

She was a sheriff's deputy. She couldn't rush in to save him from every problem. It would only get them both in trouble.

So she didn't answer.

The first time.

After the ringing paused, only to immediately begin ringing again, she sighed and did the inevitable. Maybe one of these days all the steps she'd taken to try to insulate herself from this need to be his—or anyone's—savior would actually work.

But not tonight.

She closed her eyes, let her head flop back onto the pillow and took a deep breath. "Ry, what is it?"

"I need your help."

She counted to three, inhaled deeply. Let it out. He didn't *sound* high, but that didn't mean anything. "We've been over this."

"Chloe, you don't understand. This is serious. It wasn't me. I don't know what to do. There's bones. It wasn't me. It's too old. Too deep. Chlo, I don't know what to *do*."

Panicked, clearly. But *bones* didn't make sense. She pushed up into a sitting position on the bed, tried to clear her mind. "What do you mean, Ry? I don't understand."

"By the barn. I've been digging for that new addition, right?"

She didn't say what she wanted to: *At two in the morning?* She let him blabber on only half making sense. At least it was just some jumbled talk about bones, not actual trouble with the law.

"You have to come. What am I supposed to do? I didn't do this. This isn't mine. It's *bones*."

Chloe went over everything her therapist had told her. It wasn't her job to clean up Ry's messes. He had to be responsible for his own choices.

But this wasn't the *exact* same thing. He wasn't in a fight with someone. He wasn't asking her to get him out of a ticket or an arrest. He'd just stumbled upon some bones—animal, probably—and convinced himself, perhaps with the aid of an illegal substance, it was a bigger deal than it was.

If she went over there, told him everything was fine, he'd stop bothering her for a few days. "Fine. Listen. I'll come over. But just to look at these bones, okay? But you have to stay put. And sober."

There was a pause on the other end of the line.

"I mean it, Ry. Not even a sip of beer. If I can't trust you to—"

"Okay. I promise. Nothing. Nothing else. If you just come over. Quick. I don't know what to do."

"Just don't move, and don't touch anything. Or *take* anything," she muttered, before hitting End and tossing her phone onto the empty side of the bed.

This was what her therapist didn't understand. Sometimes going over to help was the better course of action. She'd nip it in the bud and then be free of him for a few days. Best all around.

Best or easiest?

She groaned.

"Bad news?"

She didn't jolt, didn't open her eyes right away. She'd woken to an empty bed, so she figured he'd gone, because that was how this worked. Usually, that caused an ache around her heart, one she was determined to stop and never did—but tonight, him still being here was the last thing she wanted.

Just another one of her very own choices she had to face. She opened her eyes.

Jack Hudson stood, leaning his shoulder against the doorframe of her bedroom. He was dressed now, in the clothes they'd left work in: Khakis that weren't so perfectly pressed like they had been all through his workday. A Sunrise Sheriff's Department polo—untucked now.

But she knew what he looked like without all those clothes. *Hot.*

Maybe his hair was a little rumpled, but no one would think or even believe that it was *sex*-rumpled hair. Jack Hudson, the upstanding sheriff and uptight head of the

Hudson clan, engaging in a clandestine affair with one of his deputies? *Impossible*.

She still hadn't spoken, and now she watched as Tiger wound her way between Jack's long legs like she always did. Because that animal was just as foolish and weak as she was when it came to Jack.

"Chloe," he said in that half-empathetic, half-scolding tone.

He only ever used her first name *here*, what they were—and weren't—perfectly compartmentalized. Her fault as much as his, she knew, though she wished she could blame him and his rigid personality. But she'd put up walls to save herself too.

Because she was self-aware enough to know he could emotionally crush her if she didn't. She didn't think *he* knew that, and that was all that mattered.

"Just my brother. Needs me to come check something out. Typical." She slid out of bed, pulled on some sweats and put her smartwatch on her wrist. But Jack didn't leave.

She shoved her phone in her pocket. Keys and shoes were out in her living room. So she moved for the door, but Jack still stood there. Blocking her exit.

"You should head home," she told him. "A bit late for you."

He didn't say anything for a few moments as he studied her in nothing more than the glow of her smoke detector. They were shadows to each other, and yet it felt like—per usual—Jack Hudson could see *everything*.

"I'm coming with," he finally said.

Not *Would you like me to? Can I? Should I?* Not for Jack Hudson. "Not necessary, Sheriff." She threw that one at him when she wanted him to back off. Usually, it worked.

He didn't budge.

"It's two in the morning."

"Yeah."

"It's your brother."

"Yeah."

"I'm going with. We can either drive together or I can follow you, but I'm going."

"And be seen together at this hour?"

He didn't say anything. But he didn't move. Because no, Jack Hudson didn't relent. He was who he was.

Sometimes she thought she was as bad as her brother. Jack was her drug, and she couldn't give him up. Because he wasn't good for her—the secrecy; the way she couldn't get past that impenetrable, taciturn wall. But the way he made her feel when he put his hands on her was worth it.

She sighed, and she didn't relent, but Jack seemed to read the surrender in that sigh.

"I'll drive," he said, turning toward her front door.

"Of course you will," she muttered, and didn't bother to argue. She just made sure Tiger didn't bolt out the door with them in a shameless effort to follow Jack.

Chloe might be a mess, but she knew better than to throw herself against a brick wall that wasn't budging.

JACK HUDSON WAS well aware of his reputation. He knew what just about everyone thought of him. It varied a bit. To some people—particularly the law-abiding citizens of Sunrise, Wyoming—he was a saint. That was how he'd won the election for sheriff time and time again. To others—usually criminals and people related to him—he was an uptight ass.

Jack knew he was no saint, but he didn't quite agree with his siblings. Maybe he was a little strict, a little more controlled than *completely* necessary. But hey, they'd all some-how made it into adulthood in one piece and were mostly successful, and that was because of *him*.

He'd held the family together after his parents' disap-pearance when he was eighteen. He'd created Hudson Sib-ling Solutions to ensure his siblings always had jobs and to help other people with unsolved cold cases—solving quite a few, thank you.

Though never his own.

His parents—good, upstanding ranchers not involved in anything shady, that anyone had ever found—had disap-peared on a camping "date weekend" one night seventeen years ago. Just vanished.

All these years later, hours and hours of police work, private investigator work, research from every single mem-ber of his family, no one had ever discovered even a shred of evidence of what had happened to Dean and Laura Hud-son.

He told himself, day in and day out, that it was over. There would never be answers, and sometimes a man just had to accept the hard facts of life.

He was also an expert in denial.

The woman in his passenger seat, case in point. Chloe Brink hadn't *always* been a problem. Or maybe she had been and he'd just been younger and delusional. Hard to say now.

They'd been engaging in this whole *thing* for a year now, and he didn't relish the secrecy. It was an irritating neces-sity. But one of the short list of positives was that this was something his siblings had no idea about and, therefore, no say in, no opinions.

Everything that happened with Chloe was *all* his.

"Don't worry," Chloe said in the dark cab of his truck as he slowed down to take the turn into the Brink Ranch entrance. "Even if Ry said something about us arriving together in the middle of the night, no one would believe him. Or at least, not believe the real reasons."

Jack didn't respond, though it required him to grind his teeth together.

He knew she didn't understand his determination to keep this a secret. He'd never tried to explain it to her because she wouldn't believe it. In her mind, he was embarrassed, and he knew her well enough—whether *she* wanted to admit it or not—that it stemmed from her own issues. It took a lot to be a cop in the same place where your last name was pretty much synonymous with *criminal*.

Hell, wasn't that part of why he liked her so much? He wouldn't say they were too alike outside their profession. Chloe was fun and friendly. No one had ever accused him of being either. Not since he was a teenager anyway.

But they both shared a dogged determination to see through whatever they thought was right.

What she would never understand—partly because of that dogged determination and a thick skull—was that people knowing about their…relationship…would cause problems for both of them.

He'd been around enough to know she'd bear the brunt of any negative reaction to their…relationship. It wasn't fair, it wasn't right, but it wouldn't matter what she did. Or what *he* did to try to protect her.

She was a woman, and she'd get the short end of the stick when it came to their work reputations. Right or not, police work—especially police work out here in rural Wyoming—

was still male dominated. Jack dealt with the public enough to know a lot of people were still stuck in the Dark Ages.

He wouldn't let Chloe get a bad rap all because he… He was weak when it came to her, and that was *his* fault. He'd be damned if he let her take the fall for that.

So it had to be a secret, but that didn't mean he didn't care or was *embarrassed* of her.

It also didn't mean he had to like it.

Jack Hudson was well-versed in all the things he didn't like but dealt with anyway.

He pulled through the open gate to the old Brink place. It was open at a crooked angle and clearly had been that way for a while, as grass and vines had grown up and twined around it.

He didn't say anything about that either. Chloe's family was her business, and *maybe* he'd on *occasion* mentioned something about her brother, this ranch and so on, but she always put him in his place.

When he pulled up to the house, Ry was standing out in front of it, pacing back and forth. Jack could see the look on his face in the harsh light of the porch—just a light bulb screwed into the wall, no cover.

Ry was all nerves. Worry. Concern. But something was missing, and he'd dealt with Ry enough in a professional capacity to find it interesting. Chloe's little brother, for once, didn't look guilty.

Yeah, interesting.

"Why'd you bring him?" Ry asked on a whisper when they got out of the truck. Not quiet enough for Jack to miss it, but he pretended he had.

"What's the emergency, Ry?" Chloe asked, sounding

less like a sister and more like a cop—but if she was thinking with her cop brain, she wouldn't be here.

"It wasn't anything to do with me. I just found it," Ry said, louder this time, making sure Jack heard it.

Jack studied Ry Brink. No doubt he'd been high at some point today, but whatever he'd been on was wearing off. He was jittery, gray faced. Scared.

Chloe's expression was blank. "Show us," she said. She switched on a flashlight Jack hadn't realized she'd grabbed on their way out, so he figured he could turn on the one he'd gotten out of his truck as well.

Ry leaned close; this time whatever he whispered to Chloe was lost in the sound of insects buzzing and breezes sliding through the dilapidated buildings.

"Show us," she repeated, whatever Ry had said clearly not winning her over.

Ry led them away from the house, which had seen better decades. They quietly moved toward a caved-in barn. Ry. Chloe. Jack.

It was his desire to take over, to lead the way, but he tamped it down. Because this was Chloe's deal, no matter how little he liked it, and he'd only come along to ensure her brother wasn't laying some kind of trap.

Chloe might not think Ry capable, but Jack had spent his entire adult life seeing what drugs did to seemingly reasonable people. Part and parcel with a life in law enforcement.

They walked for a while in silence, and Jack noticed as they came around the side of the barn that there was a battery-powered lantern sitting in the dirt, tipped over, like it had been dropped there.

"I had this idea that I'd dig out a new entrance to the cellar," Ry said. And if he was telling the truth, it was clear he'd been high when he'd had that idea, because that wasn't going to work.

"The first one I hit, I figured it was animal. Dad used to bury the dogs out here. You remember, Chloe?"

She didn't say anything. She pointed her flashlight beam on the unearthed dirt. A shovel lay haphazardly next to the pile.

"Then I got a few more and… It's not animal bones. I know animals. It ain't animals."

Jack didn't believe that. Lots of people mistook bigger bones for human. He approached the hole with Chloe, shined his light at the ground as well.

He sucked in a breath. Heard Chloe do the same.

Human. Definitely. A full skeleton, almost. Jack swept his flashlight beam down the bones, his mind already turning with next steps. They'd have to notify Bent County. The Brink Ranch was a little outside Sunrise's jurisdiction—and besides that, they didn't have the labs or professional capacity to deal with dead bodies.

It might not be nefarious. Ranchers back in the day buried their kin on property. There were laws against such things now, but it didn't mean people always abided by them. This could be anything. It didn't have to be criminal.

Still, Jack studied the skeletal remains with an eye toward foul play. Hard not to. He swept his beam back up and noticed that something glittered. He didn't want to touch anything, destroy the scene any more than Ry already had, but he trained his light on that glitter and crouched so he could study it closer.

And it felt like the earth turned upside down, like every atom of oxygen in his body evaporated. He saw dark spots for a moment.

Chloe crouched next to him, put her hand on his back. "Jack? Are you okay? What is it?"

He had to breathe, but it was hard to suck in air. When he spoke, he heard how strangled he sounded. But he said what needed saying: "I recognize that ring."

Chloe peered closer. "How?"

"It was my mother's."

Chapter Two

Chloe figured she'd heard him wrong. She had to have heard him wrong. But he stood abruptly and took hard strides away from the remains. She was frozen, looking down at the skeleton in the beam of her flashlight. She tried to process what he was saying.

Because it couldn't be. Of all the crazy, impossible, terrible things this *might* be, it couldn't be that.

But she saw the ring, and Jack Hudson was not a jump-to-conclusions guy. He didn't say any random thought he had. The man plotted out his life to the millisecond. Even in crisis.

If he said that the little glitter of gold and diamond there in the dirt was his mother's, she believed him.

Oh God.

She stood up about as abruptly as he had. Crossed to him. There were so many…so many horrible revolving pieces to this. And she somehow had to find a path through.

For him. "Jack."

"I'll call it in," he said roughly.

"Jack—"

But he shook her off and lifted his cell to his ear. He'd have to call in Bent County. To get a dig team, the coroner. Who'd likely have to call in a forensics team from somewhere farther afield.

Chloe's mind was whirling. Too many things at once. She had to focus. Tap into cop brain. She'd been through a million crises in the past six years of being a cop. She knew how to compartmentalize.

A seventeen-year-old cold case's first huge lead being your boss slash hookup buddy's mother's bones on your family's property?

Okay, the situation was new.

"They'll send out the detectives, a few deputies to zone it off. Get in touch with the coroner," Jack said.

"Gracie Cooper. We know her. She's good." Which, it wouldn't matter if she wasn't. She was the Bent County coroner. But it seemed a tangible thing to hold on to.

"There'll be a lot of questions for Ry."

"He'll hold up," Chloe said, with far more confidence than she felt when it came to her brother. But she'd make sure she kept him in her sight, and as long as she did that, she could make certain he held up.

Right now he was pacing from Jack's truck to some point just beyond, then back again. He raked his hands through his hair. He muttered to himself.

But he didn't run. She'd give him that in this moment. While keeping an eye on him to make sure it stayed that way.

Chloe didn't let her mind go to all the things this could mean. She didn't ask herself why—why now, why here, why anything. She focused on the next steps.

Jack would need to go tell his family. He could wait for some clearer confirmation. After all, that ring—even if it had been his mother's—wasn't irrefutable proof the skeleton belonged to Laura Hudson.

Chloe had to suck in a careful breath. She could still picture the woman all these years later. Because Mrs. Hudson had been the kindergarten-room mom since Chloe had been in class with Mary, Jack's little sister. Laura had embodied everything a mother *should* be, and nothing Chloe had ever seen a mother be, so she'd been fascinated.

But worse than that memory was the fact that this discovery affected not just Jack but also Mary, one of her closest friends. Anna, their other sister. All those Hudsons.

They'd worked so hard, but the answers had always eluded them. And Chloe had never considered what it might mean—good and horrendously awful—if they finally got them.

She looked at Jack in the shadowy dark. No matter what it meant, he shouldn't be here. He needed to be with his family.

"I'll oversee this, then have Ry drive me back to my place. You go home."

"We both know your brother's license is suspended. You're not having him drive you anywhere."

"Fine. I'll have someone appropriately licensed drive me home."

Jack shook his head. Stubborn no matter what. "I don't like that."

"You've got bigger things to deal with." He'd want to tell his family before anyone got word of this. He *needed* to.

He swallowed, looked hard into the dark—the opposite direction from where that set of bones lay in the ground.

The ground of *her* family's ranch.

Would he be okay driving home on his own? Even if it wasn't confirmed, it was *possible* that this was his mother. He probably shouldn't be driving anywhere by himself.

This is Jack Hudson you're talking about. Still, the idea

of him driving by himself back to the Hudson Ranch after this… It didn't settle right.

"Maybe one of your brothers—"

"I can handle a two-mile drive." He snapped it out like an order. Boss to subordinate. But that wasn't really him, even when they *were* working, so she just nodded.

He needed to feel in control. She wasn't going to take that away from him in this moment. This horrible, awful, impossible moment.

"Then go," she told him. Because he didn't need to see the whole production once Bent County got out here. He didn't need to *see* any of this.

Still, he hesitated. She couldn't begin to imagine all the reasons he might have, but she reached out and put her hand on his shoulder. Friend to friend. Coworker to coworker. And, okay, whatever else they were when no one was around.

"Go. I've got this. You trust Deputy Brink to do her job. That's who I am right now."

His gaze finally met hers, dark. She couldn't read whatever lurked there—because he knew how to hide. Right in plain sight. Wasn't that the crux of so many of her problems with this man?

"I trust *you*, Chloe. Period," he muttered. Then he sighed, big and deep. "Promise me."

She could have pretended to misunderstand, but she knew him all too well. "I promise I won't let Ry drive me anywhere. Go. Be with your family. I'll get you an update once I have one."

She thought he might argue some more, but there was one indisputable fact about Jack Hudson. No matter how uptight, no matter how controlling, no matter how *everything*, his family came first.

So he walked back to his truck and went to them.

JACK WELCOMED THE numb feeling that settled over him. Numbness was better than pain, and pain was pointless until he had real answers. Even then...

If he thought he could hide this situation from his siblings until he had confirmation, he would have. But with Bent County involved, there were just too many ways the whispers would start.

And come knocking on the door of the Hudson Ranch.

So he drove home in the middle of the night, not sure how everything had just flipped on him. His entire adult life, suddenly different.

If that skeleton was his mother...

It wasn't a shock in that she was dead. He'd known both his parents had to be. There was no way they had disappeared on purpose. They'd been good parents, good people. They never would have left their six kids alone and defenseless.

Not on purpose.

So Jack and his siblings had known for a very long time that even if they ever found answers, there was no happy ending to this story.

But Jack had never fully realized, in all these years, how there had still been this awful bubble of hope inside him. A stray thought that they might be alive. That there might be a reason that wasn't terrible.

This strange little dream he might see them again someday.

And now that hope was gone.

It would take time to match the bones to his mother. It

would take more time to filter through all the evidence. So they were dealing in unknowns for a while yet, and Jack was no fan of dealing with those.

But in a place the size of Sunrise, with a cold case that still lingered in the town's entire identity—in the Hudson family's entire identity—he couldn't hold off going to his siblings with the facts.

He had to tell them the possibilities.

He didn't drive his truck to the outbuilding where they parked their vehicles. He parked right out front of the main house and was greeted by a couple of Cash's dogs. He didn't crouch to pet them like he usually did. He went straight for the front door, punched in the security code and then stepped inside.

The house was dark and quiet, but only for a moment. He heard a stair creak, and then the hall light came on, illuminating Mary. She was the oldest of his two younger sisters but still eight years younger than him. He'd been an adult when their parents disappeared. Well, eighteen. She'd been ten.

And still she'd stepped up. She'd helped with meals, with keeping school paperwork organized. As she'd gotten older, she'd taken on most of the administrative tasks of running Hudson Sibling Solutions *and* the Hudson Ranch.

"What are you doing up?" he asked.

She put a hand over her ever-growing stomach. Pretty soon there'd be another baby around here. Such a strange twist and turn of fate these past few years. Marriages and babies and *adulthood* for his younger siblings, far beyond what Jack had ever found for himself.

He'd been keeping as busy as possible lately to keep from thinking too much about that.

"I was up using the bathroom for the hundredth time and heard the alarm disengage and the door open. It's four in the morning. Did something come up?"

It would be easy to lie to Mary. Being sheriff gave him the perfect alibi for everything, but Mary tended to see right through him. And really, there was no point in putting her off. This had to be done.

"Yes, something came up that we all need to discuss."

He watched her hand tighten on the banister, but no sense of foreboding showed on her face. "What is it?" she asked calmly.

He couldn't tell her it wasn't serious like he wanted to. This was incredibly serious. "No one's in danger. But this is important. For all of us. Once everyone wakes up—"

"It seems like this is something that requires waking everyone up."

"It won't change anything. To wait."

Mary studied him for a few seconds. "Then it won't change anything to wake everyone up." She turned then, not waiting for him to agree or disagree.

Jack didn't follow, but slowly and quietly—no doubt for the sake of the still-sleeping kids, since his family usually didn't do anything quietly—his siblings began to arrange themselves in the living room.

Once everyone had settled, Mary nodded at him. She stood leaning against her husband, and Anna stood next to hers as well. Grant and Dahlia sat on the couch next to Cash. Carlyle stood behind Cash, clasping his hand at his shoulder. Palmer and Louisa settled themselves on an armchair.

Jack had gotten used to being a solitary figure long before his siblings had all coupled up. He'd been the man of the house. In charge. He'd needed that separation. To not be their brother anymore but to be the adult. To be in charge so he could keep everyone together until they were old enough to go on their own.

No one had. Oh, Grant had gone off to war; Mary to college; Palmer and Anna, the rodeo for a bit—but they'd all come back home. They'd all come back.

And now, in this moment, he was the only one who knew this terrible thing, and it killed him because he wanted to keep it that way. So his siblings would never have to feel this.

But it just wasn't possible. So he jumped right in. "There was a body uncovered on the Brink Ranch. It had been there for some time. Bent County will take on the investigation and attempt to identify the body, determine a cause of death."

"Why'd you wake us all up to tell us this, Jack?" Anna asked. With the kind of gravity like she knew exactly why.

"There was a ring with the remains. I recognized it right away. Mom's wedding ring."

There was a moment of complete and utter silence, everyone absorbing those words. Then Jack watched as every single member of his family turned to each other. Mary buried her head in her husband Walker's chest. Anna turned away, but Hawk pulled her back into an embrace. Louisa wound her arms around Palmer's waist, Cash's grip on Carlyle's hand tightened, and Dahlia rested her head on Grant's shoulder.

Jack tried to swallow the obstruction in his throat to ensure his voice was calm and clear. It came out rusty. "This is not incontrovertible proof, but it's—"

"What about Dad?" Anna demanded. Her voice was harsh, but there were tears in her eyes.

"I don't have any answers, Anna. All I have is a ring." He thought that admission might break him in two, but when his heart kept beating and his breath kept filling his lungs, he figured he'd survive. "Deputy Brink is handling it. We all know we can trust her to handle it."

"Except this was found on her family's ranch?" Palmer said, no doubt echoing some people's thoughts on the matter.

But Jack didn't need to defend Chloe. Mary did it first.

"That doesn't mean anything," she said, standing up for her friend. "I trust Chloe. No matter what."

"The Brinks—"

Carlyle cut off whatever Palmer was going to say. No doubt something about the Brinks and their connection to crime, drugs and a hell of a lot of trouble.

"The Bent County detectives will be the ones handling it, right?" Carlyle asked. "Hart and Laurel? They'll be doing the investigation, and we all know they're damn good at their jobs."

Thomas Hart and Laurel Delaney-Carson had worked with Cash and Carlyle a few months back, and their hard work had helped keep Cash from being blamed for his ex-wife's murder. Hart had also been involved in helping to solve a case last year when someone had tried to kill Anna.

They were both good detectives, and Jack trusted them. He had to.

"We'll be investigating too," Anna said.

"No," Jack said firmly, looking at his baby sister and the stubborn set of her chin. "We're staying out of this."

All eyes turned to him, surprise slackening every single person's features.

"Jack. You can't be serious," Grant said in his quiet way.

But Jack was very serious. He'd made this decision the minute he'd driven off the Brink Ranch. "This is a Bent County investigation. We will stay out of their way and let them investigate. There's nothing for us to do here."

"Do you have a head injury?" Anna demanded. "This is our parents we're talking about. *Our* seventeen-year-old cold case. Why the hell would we stay out of the way now that we actually have a lead?"

"Maybe once we have all the facts, we can decide to pursue it. But for now, we wait. Because none of us need to be involved in the details of our parents' remains." No one in this room needed to see what he'd seen tonight, needed to have that haunting them for the rest of their days.

For years, they'd tried to come up with clues to follow when it came to their parents' disappearance. For years, they'd gone over the campsite. Their parents' pasts. Anything and everything. That had seemed innocent enough. Important enough that they could all be in on the investigating.

But nothing had involved bodies. Nothing had involved the reality of their parents being dead. Not just dead— *bones*.

No. None of them needed to see it. "We'll give Bent County the space to handle the investigation. There's going to be talk around town. People will want to know what we think. I want us to be as quiet about it as we can until we know for sure what we're dealing with. Because we don't know yet. All we know is, we've uncovered a ring that used to be our mother's."

For a moment, that old hope tried to grow back, but he ruthlessly plucked that weed of a thought.

His parents were dead, and it was someone else's job to figure out how. And why.

Chapter Three

Chloe was bone tired, but a text or a phone call wasn't going to cut it. Not for this.

She hadn't been back home. When the police had arrived at the ranch, she'd stayed through everything. Even when it became clear what they were dealing with, and someone pointed out that Chloe was one of the landowners.

The detectives hadn't liked that, but she knew enough to avoid anyone hauling her off the property. Just like she knew enough to keep Ry from being hauled off too. Once she'd gotten as much out of Bent County officers as she knew she was going to get, she'd driven Ry back to her cabin and insisted he stay put.

She didn't know if he'd listen, but it didn't matter. She had to drive back out to the Hudson Ranch and update the family.

Eventually, Bent County would get around to filling them in, but they were likely still organizing information. Chloe had to get in and tell the Hudsons some things before Bent County did so the Hudsons could organize.

Jack probably had a plan in place already, but he didn't know…

Chloe pulled up to the main house on the Hudson Ranch with nothing but dread in her stomach. She was used to delivering bad news. It went hand in hand with the job. And in a town like Sunrise, she was often delivering bad news to people she knew and liked.

But this was different. On so many levels. Complicated levels. And she just didn't know how to arrange it all behind her usual cop facade.

She got out of her car and trudged toward the porch. She'd been to the Hudson house for a variety of reasons over the years, but never for the reason Jack came to her place. Set lines. Set boundaries. Ones she'd helped enact because she'd thought it would somehow keep her safe from all her soft feelings.

It hadn't, and she didn't like to be reminded of that. She straightened her shoulders, knocked on the door. She'd changed into her Sunrise SD polo and put on her badge in an attempt to *feel* official on the outside since she didn't feel it on the inside.

Mary answered. She was dressed for the day, prim and proper as usual, even with her big pregnant belly. She was clearly tired, though, but Chloe wasn't about to tell her that.

"Aren't you pretty."

Mary's smile was faint, and she rolled her eyes. "I'm puffy and exhausted and ready to be done. I'm guessing this isn't a social call," she said, nodding at Chloe's badge.

Chloe tried to keep her smile in place as she shook her head. "No, I thought I'd update you all before Bent County swoops in."

Mary nodded. "Come on. We're all in the dining room." Mary led her deep into the house. Normally, there would have been lots of conversation, arguing, shouts and dogs barking echoing through the house before Chloe even got close to the dining room.

This morning it was silent. When she entered the room, the only sound was the scraping of forks on plates, though she wasn't sure anyone was eating a lot.

The table was full, everyone—and there was a *lot* of *everyone* at this house—taking a seat. Paired up with their significant others. Cash's twelve-year-old flanked between him and Carlyle. Anna's baby tucked into her husband's arm.

And Jack, sitting at the head of the table. Surrounded by his family, and yet he looked so alone.

There was a chorus of unsure greetings from the table when Mary announced her arrival. Chloe refused a seat and a plate. "I just came to give you all a few updates. I'll be out of your hair in a few minutes."

It wasn't pure cowardice. She wanted to get out before Bent County showed up and asked why she was here. Besides, she had a shift to work.

"Izzy and I are going to go handle the dog chores," Carlyle said, her hand on Cash's twelve-year-old daughter's shoulder.

Chloe half expected the girl to argue. Even she knew Izzy didn't like to be shuffled off, but it seemed there'd already been discussion and agreement since she disappeared with Carlyle to take care of Cash's dogs without argument.

"Go on, then," Jack said, not unkindly but with that stoic detachment of his firmly in place.

"Another set of remains was found next to the first." Chloe had to resist the urge to clear her throat, but she couldn't resist the urge to look at Jack, to try to see what he was really feeling under that mask of stoicism.

Mostly, she figured no one would see that lost look to his

dark eyes. They'd see the grim expression, the hard line of his mouth, and think he had it under control.

He didn't. Chloe knew he didn't, and she knew he'd die before admitting it to anyone. Even himself.

"Any identifying information?" he asked.

"They wouldn't tell me anything, but I took a slightly illegal and unauthorized picture of some evidence they gathered. I can show whoever is willing to bend the rules a little bit what I've got."

Immediately, most of the Hudsons crowded around her as she took out her phone. She pulled the picture up on the screen and tried not to betray her surprise when Jack stepped close enough in front of her to see it as well.

"You already saw one ring, Jack, but there was a ring with the other remains as well. They're both in this evidence bag." She zoomed in on the picture so they could see the rings.

Then she looked up at Jack. He didn't have to say anything. Chloe could see it in his eyes.

He nodded.

Chloe knew it would be Dean Hudson's wedding band, but maybe she'd hoped... Oh, she didn't know. There was very little possibility the two skeletal remains weren't the missing Hudson parents.

She had to remind herself to look away from Jack, to focus on her job. "The detectives will be by to fill you guys in. To ask questions, I'm sure. I...tried to convince them to let me, but it was a no go."

"It's best if it's a third party," Jack said. "We're all staying out of it, letting Bent County do their job."

Chloe opened her mouth to say something, but she forgot what because that didn't make *any* sense. "I'm sorry. What?"

"See?" Anna muttered. "Staying out of it doesn't make any sense."

But Jack's expression remained firm, and he didn't look at Anna. "Thanks for the update, Deputy Brink, but we think—"

"*You* think," Palmer interjected.

"—it's best if we let police handle this."

"Oh. Well, sure." She had just been resoundingly dismissed. She was so shocked by it, so confused by Jack's unusual response, she just stood there for a moment, not quite sure what to do.

"Are you sure you don't want any breakfast, Chloe?" Mary asked.

Chloe shook her head. No. She needed to leave. She needed… She glanced at Jack. He was calmly sipping from his coffee mug. But she recognized those careful, mild movements.

They were very deliberate. Very *careful*, like he was holding himself braced for a blow. He'd looked like that when Louisa had been kidnapped last year, when Anna had been in the hospital—basically any time a member of his family was in trouble, it was like there was a ticking time bomb inside he was doing everything he could not to detonate.

And it was *none* of her business. "Well, I'm heading into my shift. I'll…" She didn't know what to say if they didn't want insider updates on the whole thing. Well, not *they*. Jack.

But Jack ran the show. This time she had to clear her throat in order to speak. "I'll see you all later."

She turned on a heel, and she had no idea why she felt

emotional. And just so very, very alone. But she walked out of the house having to work way too hard to fight back tears.

She just needed rest. After she worked her shift, she'd sleep. Of course, first she'd have to deal with what she was going to do with her brother. Which was a whole other headache she didn't have any answers for.

Before she could reach the bottom of the porch stairs, she heard Jack say her name.

She closed her eyes and sucked in a breath. Repeated her *Be strong* mantra a few times before she turned to face him.

"Thank you for coming out," he said, a little stiffly. "We appreciate the update."

She couldn't help but be amused despite everything churning inside her. She knew them all a little too well. "Mary made you come say that."

One side of his mouth *almost* curved. "My siblings can't *make* me do anything."

"But she did. Because she's Mary, and *she* can make you do things. Especially when she's that pregnant."

He shrugged, not refuting it. He squinted out at the mountains, the pretty Hudson Ranch, and didn't say anything. But he didn't leave either.

And she knew he *shouldn't* since he had all that family under his very own roof, but she could see the loneliness on him. Because like recognized like.

"They'll run tests," she said reassuringly. Maybe she didn't understand the hands-off stance he was taking, but she wanted him to know it was handled. "They'll do what they can to determine when. How."

"I know how it works, Chloe."

It was ridiculous the little thrill she got out of this man calling her by her first name when he damn well *should*.

It wasn't like they were at work. "Sometimes it's good to hear someone else say what you already know."

He didn't say anything to that, and she knew she should go. *Had* to get out of here soon. But she just couldn't step away from him when he seemed so alone.

"They're not going to let me within a hundred feet of this case since my name is on the deed of the land. They've already questioned Ry. I'll be next."

"What about your parents?"

She shrugged, trying not to go on the defensive. He had every right to ask that question. Hell, *she'd* asked that question. "I imagine they'll do that too. But they'll have to get down to Texas to visit Dad in prison—and if they have better luck tracking down my mother than I ever have, more power to them. I'll be first because I'm here. Because I was there."

"I was there with you."

"I didn't mention it."

"Chloe. I called it in."

She shrugged. "You can always say I called you first and then you called it in."

"Why would I lie about that?"

"You know why, Jack."

"I know why *you* think I should lie, but I don't think you have any clue what *I* think."

She had no business getting pissed at him over relationship stuff. Mostly because she was just as much to blame for *everything* involved in this, but also because now so clearly wasn't the time.

But she was tired, and she was feeling all emotional over too many things to count, and *he* was the one who'd brought it up. So she snapped. "Oh, really? Then enlighten me. What does the almighty Jack Hudson think?"

"You think it's because I'm embarrassed. Because of your family or because I'm your boss."

"That's not embarrassing, Jack. It's unethical. Something you are historically very opposed to." She looked up at him to give him a kind of *so there* smirk, but his expression was serious, his gaze steady, and when he spoke, he spoke with all the gravity of the truth.

"I'm not embarrassed of you, Chloe. Not in the least."

Her foolish heart felt as though it actually skipped a beat. Was she really this pathetic?

Yes, yes you are. When it comes to him, you always have been.

She swallowed, trying to find some retort that would settle all this terrible longing inside her, but she heard the sound of a car approaching and turned toward it.

Not just any car. A Bent County cruiser was driving up the gravel road when Chloe had been planning to get out of here before they showed up. Because no doubt the detectives were inside.

"Damn," she muttered.

"Don't worry. I'm going to protect you, Chloe," Jack said, like that made any sense. But before she could ask him what on earth he was talking about, he was striding forward to meet the detectives.

JACK DEALT WITH the detectives. He didn't lie to them about being with Chloe when her brother called, but he didn't explain either. Since the detectives were more concerned with identifying the remains, keeping Sunrise SD out of the proceedings and the Brink family connection to the

Hudson family, they didn't prod for answers. It wasn't relevant to the case.

He wouldn't let it be. He'd protect her reputation. No matter what.

The detectives didn't share any breaking new information. Next steps were with the forensic anthropologist and the assurance that all the Brinks would be questioned.

He might have balked at that, but at the end of the day, it was clear the remains had been in the ground for some time. Long enough that Chloe and Ry would have been kids when it happened. Maybe the detectives thought they'd seen something, heard something, would remember something from back then, but Jack doubted it.

First, Chloe would have said long ago. And even Ry didn't seem like the type who could keep his mouth shut about much. That's half of why he got in so much trouble. No criminal mastermind, there. Just a kid with no direction who'd gotten mixed up with drugs.

It amazed him, regularly, that Chloe had somehow come out of all that to be the good cop and good person she was.

She'd left pretty quickly after the detectives had arrived, having to get to her shift, and Jack had taken the detectives inside, working with Mary to gather all the information they had on their parents' case. He handed over years' worth of files.

"You don't want to make copies?" Laurel asked with a raised eyebrow.

"We have most of this stuff digitized, but we're happy to hand over anything that might help you get to the bottom of this." He ignored the disapproving look on Mary's face.

Hart looked from Mary to Jack, a handful of files now

in his grasp. "It's going to be best if you guys stay out of it for now."

Jack nodded. "We plan to."

"You forget I've had to deal with your family before, Sheriff," Laurel offered with a smile, as if to put some kind of friendly spin on things. Jack didn't particularly feel like being friendly.

"I've made it clear to my family our best course of action is to step back and let you all do your job. I can't promise they'll listen, but I'll do my best to control the situation." That was what he'd done for the past seventeen years. No reason to stop now.

Hart and Laurel shared a look, clearly not believing him. But they didn't press the matter.

"We'll keep you as informed as we can. We're going to be looking into the disappearance again, but no real answers can come until the forensic anthropologist gives us a report. We don't have a timetable on that."

Jack nodded. He'd never dealt with a case like this, so he wasn't fully abreast of the procedure, but he knew the general proceedings when anyone had to call in outside agencies for help. No doubt it would be a long, drawn-out process. Even more reason for his family to stay out of it. Focus on the lives they were building, cases that needed their attention, the ranch.

Mary showed the detectives back out, and Jack tried not to think about how long this was going to drag out. How much he was going to have to deal with the speculation at work. How difficult it was going to be to keep his family reined in.

But difficult was the name of the game, wasn't it? It wasn't like things had been particularly easy lately. Sure, his siblings had paired off, some of them starting families, but there had been danger and threat at every turn.

No rest for the wicked.

And still, he just stood in the office where they kept their paper files and stared blankly at the now-empty drawer. Sixteen years of work. Research. Investigation. And he was just handing it over to two people who'd never met his parents.

Who'd never been hugged by his mother or listened to one of his father's corny jokes. People who'd never been surrounded by the love that Laura and Dean Hudson had imbued every last interaction with.

They hadn't been perfect people. He knew that. But they'd been good.

And he thought he'd grieved over it a long, long time ago.

He knew, mired in all this old grief, he was absolutely doing the right thing for his family. Maybe he couldn't save them from going through this all over again, but if he could make a buffer, a wall between them and all this old hurt, he would consider it a success.

"For the record, I may not agree fully, but I understand what you're doing."

Jack turned toward Mary, who was standing in the doorway, arms across her chest and resting on her pregnant belly. Expression disapproving even if her words were about understanding.

"What's that?"

"Trying to protect us from the harsh reality that our parents were murdered, put in a shallow grave some seventeen years ago, and we never would have found the answers if not for Ry Brink's random and likely drug-fueled decision to dig a hole."

Jack felt something inside him constrict at the tidy, emotionless way Mary laid out the truth.

"You saw something you don't want us to have to see," she continued.

He tried to block the image of that ring and bones from his mind, but he couldn't quite manage it.

"I think if you were honest about that, you'd have more of us supporting you. Even Anna might relent a little if she knew—"

"Hawk will keep her in line."

"I can't believe you just said that. Out loud. And no bolt of lightning came to strike you down like it very well should."

"I didn't mean it like that. I just mean he loves her. He'll protect her, and that means keeping her from diving head-first into all this." Not that Jack was sure he'd succeed, but Hawk was the only chance of Anna actually listening. So Jack would depend on it.

Mary was silent for a long while. "Sometimes love isn't about protecting people, Jack. Sometimes it's just about loving them." She didn't wait for him to have any answer to that. She just left.

Jack refused to engage with that sentiment. It was his normal weekend off from the sheriff's department anyway, so he went out and did some ranch chores. He went through his *normal* day, trying to shut everything off.

But it only seemed to settle deeper, tying tight, heavy knots in his gut, in his chest. Every step, every breath became harder. Every minute that ticked by seemed to be leading somewhere terrible.

Only nothing out of the ordinary happened. He had a normal dinner with his family. Well, not *normal*. There was a heavy quiet that had taken over the house today. Even baby Caroline appeared to have gotten the memo and wasn't overly fussy or energetic. No one could seem to muster a conversation that didn't immediately lull into silence.

People excused themselves earlier than usual. No one ate dessert. Jack had cleanup duty with Carlyle, whose nervous energy seemed to suck all his own energy away. Or maybe it was the fact that he hadn't really slept.

Once she'd brought all the dishes into the kitchen, she paused, staring at him. Since he'd never known her to hesitate over just about anything, he raised an eyebrow. "Something you wanted to say?"

"Cash wanted me to run it by you first, but I figure I'd tell Zeke," she said, referring to her brother *not* mixed up in the Hudson household. "He's got all those crazy connections to underground spy people. I know you want Bent County handling it, but Zeke might have a line on a good… What did they call it? Forensic person or whatever? He knows some people who could poke around, and they wouldn't get in Bent County's way."

Jack wanted to dismiss it out of hand. He wanted to dismiss everything out of hand, but the more people looking into this who weren't his family, the quicker this could move. "That'd be fine, Carlyle. Thank you for asking."

They worked in silence for a while; then, just about when they were finished and he thought he could escape to the isolation of his bedroom, Carlyle said something that stopped him in his tracks.

"Chloe's a good listener."

Jack turned his head slowly to stare at her. Her blue-gray eyes held his, but she didn't look accusatory or like she was holding some secret over his head.

She shrugged. "I just know, from experience, sometimes you don't want to, like…be a burden to your family. And I could sit here and lecture you for a million days how you're not, but it doesn't change the feeling you don't want to unload on the people also going through what you're going through."

"What does that have to do with Deputy Brink?"

Carlyle rolled her eyes. "*Chloe's* a good listener. That's all I'm saying." Then she shrugged and left the kitchen.

Leaving Jack standing there, breathing a little too hard. It wasn't concern that Carlyle knew he had a more-than-working relationship with Chloe. He'd had a bad feeling for a while that Carlyle had some inkling of what was going on between them. But she'd never come out and said anything, and Carlyle wasn't exactly *subtle*.

It was Mary's words about love. Carlyle's words about unloading on people. It was the oppressive silence in the house, like grief had tightened its ugly chains around the whole ranch once again.

He didn't want it to. That first year after losing his parents had been the hardest damn year of his life—all their lives—and he didn't want it touching any of his siblings again. Ever again.

But here it was, and he couldn't seem to breathe. Couldn't seem to find a solution. No amount of keeping them separate from the realities seemed to change what they were all feeling internally.

Sad and shaken and quiet.

Except there was something else inside him. A tightening in his chest, a struggle to breathe. The pressure of seventeen years beating down on him, like someone pounding a stake into the ground, and he was the stake.

He was half-afraid he was having some kind of cardiac event, but there was no shooting pain in his arm. No losing consciousness. Just this overwhelming *pressure*—worse but not all that different from when things went off-plan.

Panic attack.

To hell with that. Just to hell with it. He strode out of the kitchen, out the back door and toward his truck. Normally, he'd make sure someone knew where he was, but he couldn't. He just couldn't.

He had to get out, and even though he wouldn't admit to himself where he was going, it didn't surprise him to pull off onto the shoulder of the road that led up to Chloe's cabin fifteen minutes later.

He didn't turn into the driveway. He idled on the shoulder, staring at the front door. She likely had Ry in there. She wouldn't want her brother staying out at the ranch when he was unpredictable, and likely there was some police presence still. So this was a pointless endeavor. He wasn't going inside. He wasn't going to use her like some kind of crutch.

He did just fine on his own. Had for sixteen years. He'd finished raising a family. He'd built a business, been a cop, become sheriff. There wasn't anything he couldn't control. All on his own.

And still he fished his phone out of his pocket. Still he brought up a text message to Chloe.

He shouldn't do this. He knew he shouldn't. That was the wildest part of everything that had happened with Chloe since he'd let his guard down at that ridiculous party last year. She had touched him, wearing that excuse for a dress, and it had upended something inside.

Every finely tuned, rule-following, controlled, upstanding rule he'd set for himself, killed himself to follow...

He'd break, every time, when it came to her. Just like he was doing right now, typing out the text.

You want to go for a drive?

She didn't respond, but not two minutes later the door to the cabin opened, and she stepped outside. Her hair was wet, and she was wearing sweatpants and a sweatshirt, but she smiled at him and walked toward his truck, her cat in her arms.

And weirdly, he could breathe again.

Chapter Four

Chloe hopped into the passenger side of Jack's truck, Tiger in her grasp. The minute she was settled, the cat immediately escaped and made a beeline for Jack's lap.

He looked rough. Oh, he hid it well. The stoic expression. The way, somehow, even though he likely hadn't slept at all, he looked as alert and in control as he always did.

But she saw the little things. The way his hand gripped the steering wheel. The impossibly tense clench of his jaw.

She wanted to reach across and rub her palm against it until he relaxed. But she didn't. Not yet. She wasn't quite sure what this was yet. Truth be told, she was always waiting for him to drop the hammer. End this. Just because he hadn't yet didn't mean he never would.

But he had a lot more than *her* on his mind right now, and she doubted he had the mental capacity to finally come to his senses when it came to whatever they were doing.

"So, where we driving to?" She didn't explain Ry was staying at her cabin. If he hadn't already known it, he would have come up to her door.

"I… I'm not sure," he said.

Worry slithered through her. She wondered if she'd ever once heard Jack say those three words. She tried to sound cheerful and unbothered, though. An anchor to how lost he seemed. "How about up around the scenic viewpoint?"

He nodded. "Yeah, that sounds good." He started driving, never once looking over at her. He drove with one hand on the wheel and one hand on Tiger, down the highway toward the turnoff that would lead up and around one of the smaller peaks, with pretty views out over the larger mountain range as a whole.

But not long after they'd passed the main entrance to the Hudson Ranch, he took a sharp and unexpected turn off the highway. Chloe had to grab on to the dash to keep from slamming into the door.

"Uh, where are we going?"

"Just a different place I know." His expression was grim, and even though he was making her a little nervous, she didn't say anything or ask any more questions. She just sat back and tried to figure it out herself.

It was a side road, but she was pretty sure they were on Hudson property. Confirmed when they drove past Palmer's new house that he and Louisa had finished about the time they'd gotten married.

Then the road changed from gravel to dirt and started going...up. Chloe's grip on whatever she could find tightened. She looked over at Tiger, whose eyes were half-closed as if it was naptime.

Meanwhile, Chloe's throat constricted, and her entire body tensed as it began to feel like they were driving straight up. Up the mountain. Chloe didn't consider herself squeamish about much, but narrow mountain roads weren't her favorite. That was why she'd suggested the overlook—the road up to it was paved and well maintained.

When he came to a stop and shoved his truck into Park,

at such an angle gravity had her practically pressed to her door, she realized she'd been holding her breath. She let it out shakily, and Jack looked over at her.

For the first time today, she saw that grave, expression in his eyes turn to humor, which made her entire being *flutter*.

"Sorry. Forgot you get panicky about heights."

"Not panicky. Just not keen on tumbling to my death in a truck."

"Yeah, that's not panicky at all. Come on." He got out of the truck, Tiger in his arms like it was normal to carry a cat around. But for some reason, that cat looked content as could be wrapped up in Jack's arms.

Yeah, you know the feeling, don't you?

He grabbed a blanket from the back of his truck, tucked it under his free arm and then began marching toward some unknown point. He never said a word. She scurried after his long strides. She didn't mind heights when she was on her own two feet—or at least, that's what she tried to tell herself. Especially when Jack kept walking right up to the edge of what looked a hell of a lot like a cliff.

Chloe stepped very carefully behind him, but once she looked up from her feet, she stopped short.

"Jack," she breathed.

She'd seen a lot of pretty views. Sunrise and Bent County were full of them. She'd spent summers enjoying everything the Tetons and Yellowstone had to offer. She'd even gone up to Glacier with a friend from the police academy one summer. All those places had been awe-inspiring, gorgeous. It was amazing what the natural world could be.

But this was… She couldn't explain it. Not just the natural beauty of mountain and sky and land stretched out as far as the eye could see. There was something like a peaceful settling inside her. Like all her life, she'd been looking for this exact view, and now she'd finally found it.

The sun was sinking in the sky, but it wasn't sunset just yet. The world had taken on a softer, pinker hue, though. And Jack Hudson stood there, at the edge of this little out-cropping, holding her *cat*, and she knew she'd just…never get over him. Not in a million years.

One-handed, he spread out the blanket until she crouched to help him. Then they both sat down on it. The cat stayed curled in Jack's lap, definitely not about to give up comfort for the wild world around them.

This time she didn't resist the urge. She smoothed her hand down his jaw. He didn't relax, but he did turn to her. And when she wrapped her arms around him, all comfort, he accepted.

And finally, *some* of that tension left him.

Maybe when all was said and done, it wasn't the fantastic sex; it wasn't that he was so handsome or so good. It was this.

She seemed to be the only one who could comfort Jack Hudson. To ease that tension, to release some of those burdens he'd been perfecting carrying for so long. *She* had that power, and for all the ways this relationship was messed up and messy, she couldn't walk away from that.

When she pulled away, she didn't pull far. She leaned her head against his shoulder, and he rested his head atop hers while they both looked out at the sun's slow descent.

JACK DIDN'T REALLY know what he was doing. In so many different ways. He couldn't keep getting more and more mixed up with Chloe when he couldn't offer her anything except complications He didn't have time to just be *sitting* here, enjoying the feel of her head on his shoulder. There were things to do—ranch things, sheriff things, family things.

And still he sat, soaking in this moment in one of his favorite places on the ranch. The terms of his parents' will had been that he inherited the main house. The other kids had their pick of equal parcels of land once they reached eighteen, and Palmer had already staked out his. Grant was looking at one closer to the main road since Dahlia worked in town as the librarian. Mary and Anna seemed content to stay put in the main house and have their portions of land dedicated to the ranch, and Jack hoped they would always. Cash was still deciding what to do next after his cabin had been destroyed.

Jack had been in the main-floor bedroom since his parents had disappeared, and part of him figured he'd stay there till he croaked.

But he'd always secretly wanted to build a little house right here and wake up to that view every morning.

He shouldn't have brought Chloe here. She'd be part of that fantasy now too. And it was a fantasy neither of them could really afford.

Speaking of fantasies. "They're not going to listen to me, are they?"

She was quiet for a long while, and he wondered if he'd have to explain. He didn't want to. He already wished he hadn't said anything.

"I think you'd be surprised how much they'd listen to you if you were honest with them."

It made him think of Mary's little speech about love and protection. He didn't fully agree with her, but he understood a certain level of detachment in trying to hold everyone together, in trying to raise his siblings, had led to them thinking he was something of a benevolent dictator.

He didn't mind that. Maybe he even relished it a little bit since it made things easier. But it meant he'd lost the ability to know how to explain to them this was important. That his *protection* did come from love, no matter what Mary said.

"Then again, once they think about it, they'll probably figure out what you're actually doing."

"What's that?"

"Protecting them. It's what you're always doing. Everyone knows it. Sometimes you just irritate them enough with it, they can't see the forest through the trees."

"And what's the forest?"

"Love, Jack."

The word landed hard, right there at the center of his chest. He even tensed against it, and wished he hadn't because she'd no doubt feel it. But she didn't lift her head or scoot away. They sat there together. That silence wrapping around him like a cocoon, like a soft place to land.

Like the one place he could let his guard down enough to speak the truth. "I didn't realize that I still had this ridiculous hope they were still alive."

She rubbed a hand up and down his back, and he thought maybe he'd survive all this crushing weight if she kept doing that.

"Hope is the human condition," she said, a little too philosophically for his taste. But she shrugged and kept going. "No matter how many times he proves me wrong, I hope *this* time will be the time Ry gets clean, gets his life together. Sometimes I have this awful daydream that my mother comes back and wants to bake Christmas cookies together."

"Ouch."

"Yeah. Life's kind of an ouch."

"That's why I keep trying to turn into a robot."

Which made her laugh. A rare thing. Oh, she laughed with Mary, with Anna, with just about everyone. But not as much with him as he would've liked.

She lifted her head from his shoulder, stretched forward and squinted out at the sunset. Then she turned back and met his gaze.

"You're not much of an avoider, Jack. So why'd you come out here?" She didn't ask the other question that hung in the air: *Why'd you come get me?*

Which he didn't have an answer for. Not one that did them any good anyway. So he answered the one she'd voiced. "It's like all those years I did my best to clean the ghosts out of that house, and now they're all back."

"Maybe they aren't so much ghosts as…legacy."

"Is that different?"

"Sort of. You loved your parents. They loved you. You guys had—*have*—a great family because they built it on a legacy of love. That was always going to hurt when a piece of it was lost, but it's also like this…really cool thing. Because you've got Izzy and Caroline—and whatever Mary's going to name the baby, which she *refuses* to tell me even though I know they've decided. They're all getting raised in that same legacy even though they'll never get to meet the people who started it. Not everyone gets that, Jack. Which doesn't mean it's not sad or doesn't hurt, especially losing them the way you did, especially having to relive it now. It just means…sad isn't all bad. Sometimes ghosts can be a comfort instead of something to run from."

He knew a lot of people saw him as brave, strong. That

whole saint thing again. No one seemed to understand he always felt like he was running from something.

Except Chloe.

He wanted her. To come home with him, to share his bed. Not just because of sexual chemistry but also because of this. The moments where it felt like she was the only one he could lean on when he'd spent so many years refusing to lean on anyone.

She managed to find just the right access point to crack him open. He'd never understand how or why; he just knew that she did. And when he leaned on her, he didn't feel guilty or ashamed. She never let him.

Somehow it figured it'd be one of the few women in his life who was completely off-limits.

"We should get back."

She nodded, and that was that. She collected Tiger, against the cat's protests. Jack shook out the blanket, and then they walked back to his truck and drove all the way to Chloe's cabin without saying a single word.

He pulled into the drive this time, idling. She let Tiger out of the vehicle and then got out herself, but she leaned in.

"You don't have to wait for me to get in the door, Jack. I'm a big girl."

He nodded.

But he waited all the same.

Chapter Five

Chloe knew he wouldn't drive away just because she'd told him to. He'd wait until she got inside. She supposed it should irritate or frustrate her, but considering her parents hadn't cared that much about her when she'd been a *child*, she couldn't muster up taking offense to Jack's tendency to overprotect.

Hell, she didn't just not take offense—she downright loved it. She'd been taking care of herself and everyone else for as long as she could remember. She'd even dedicated her life to a job that protected other people, best she could.

Yeah, she didn't mind someone out there caring enough to protect *her* for once.

And that is why you find yourself in a dysfunctional, secret relationship.

So lost in her own thoughts, she nearly stepped on something on her porch, but she pulled her foot back in the nick of time.

A snake. Maybe two. Except not *full* snakes. Chunks. Mutilated. Chopped into pieces strewn about her pretty porch. She might have been able to convince herself it was the work of an animal except for the fact that the head of one was sticking out from one of her planters of cheerful pansies. *That* was pointed, and it made her stomach turn over a little bit.

"Call it in."

She nearly jumped a foot. She'd been caught so off guard by the snake, she hadn't heard Jack come up to see what had made her stop.

"Jack, it's a sick prank."

"Fine. I'll call it in."

She looked away from the gruesome sight and scowled at him. "Jack Hudson, you will not waste Sunrise's resources on something so pointless."

"Okay. You've called it in to me. I'll take the report. And the pictures." He patted his pockets, pulled out his phone and started taking pictures of the splattered remains.

"You're not on duty."

"I'm the sheriff. I'm always on duty."

Chloe rolled her eyes, but there was, per usual, no arguing with him. He took the pictures. He noted the time, looked around the house for footprints or tire prints that didn't belong to him or her cruiser.

Chloe went to the garage to figure out what she could use to clean it all up. Part of her wanted to make Ry do it, because God knew this probably had to do with him, but then he'd be out here with Jack, and she tried to keep them from being in the same orbit as much as she could.

Embarrassed of your own brother. What a great sister you are.

She strode into her garage, pushing away those old thoughts. Because Ry *was* embarrassing. He made bad choices she didn't approve of, and while that might not reflect on who *she* was as a person, while she might not be able to take over and stop him from those bad decisions, they *did* still affect her, and she got to have feelings about that.

She was a *damn* good sister, considering what her baby brother had put her through.

She blew out a long breath, attempting to get her rioting feelings under control. How ridiculous that they were more about Jack and her brother than chunks of mutilated snake all over her porch.

Maybe Jack was right, and this was connected to last night. If she removed all feeling from the situation, it was plausible. But there were a *lot* of plausible explanations. Especially since her brother was staying with her right now and he was a beacon for trouble.

She got a shovel, then trudged back to the front porch. For all the ways she was used to Jack taking over, it still surprised her when he tried to grab the shovel out of her hand.

"I've got it."

"I'll do it," he replied. "You just want it buried out back, right?"

There was that forever internal fight. Let someone else handle it versus handle it herself. Jack was the only one in her acquaintance whose stubbornness ever matched her own, and it had made her complacent. She didn't want to be that.

Except she didn't want to fight him. She let him take the shovel, scoop up the snake remains—he'd even gotten some gloves from his truck and picked out the one in her flowerpot. Then he buried it all while she stood there... internally arguing with herself.

And still, per usual, she came to no answers. Because Jack was...

A problem.

Once he was finished, he put the shovel away himself, not even asking her where it went. Still, she knew he'd put it in the exact right place. And there was something about the current situation—the potential that his parents had been murdered and buried on her family's ranch—that made her fully realize just what had made him this way.

She liked to think *Oh, that's just Jack Hudson*, but it was more, wasn't it? Trauma. Through and through. He'd been forced to take care of five siblings and a ranch at *eighteen*. And instead of faltering, instead of losing himself in drugs or bad behavior as her brother had with all their trauma, Jack Hudson had built himself into *this*.

It was amazing. But more than that, for the first time, she really just felt sorry for him. The pressure he must have put on himself. The sheer weight he carried on those broad shoulders and probably didn't even realize it. Probably didn't even think to share it.

Because he'd always had to do it on his own.

It made a lump form in her throat because she knew all too well what that felt like, and still she knew he'd taken on more.

When he returned to her on the porch, his expression was grim. "I want you to come stay at the ranch."

Okay, *that* was a step too far, even with all this emotion swirling around inside her. "Honestly, Jack, what do you think this is besides some bad joke? Either by one of Ry's friends or some kids whose beer I poured out last week or maybe the guy I arrested for domestic assault last month or—"

"Two skeletal remains were found on property you partially own last night, then it just so happens you get a threatening prank at your cabin today? That's enough cause. Go on inside and get Ry."

She blinked, so taken aback by all this that she felt like she'd forgotten how to fight when her whole life had been about the fight. "For what?"

"He's coming too. I'll call Mary. We'll have two rooms ready."

For a long time she could only stare at him. Ry at the Hudson Ranch? Ry with *all* the Hudsons. And her. No. "Jack, Ry isn't…"

"I know what Ry is and what he isn't," Jack returned. "You're both going to be looked after until we get to the bottom of this."

Chloe felt like she couldn't breathe. *Looked after.* It was one thing in secret. It was another thing if he was *looking after* things in front of his family. Another thing if Ry was involved.

"Jack, we can't…"

"I understand your reticence, Chloe, I do," he said, his voice low and less cop-Jack and more the Jack he only ever was when they were alone together. "But this is concerning. I can't just ignore it, and I can't just let you handle it on your own when you've got Ry and a job to contend with and this could be… We don't have the first clue what happened here or with my parents. Until we do, we have to act with all the caution in the world so no one else gets hurt."

He tried to hide it, but she could easily see all that grief he'd talked about up at the overlook there in his dark eyes, and she didn't know how to argue with that. So she went inside to tell her brother they were going to stay at the Hudson Ranch.

JACK LET CHLOE drive Ry and Tiger over to the ranch in her personal car, though it pained him. They both had a shift tomorrow, so he could drive her to her cabin on the way into Sunrise headquarters and pick up her patrol car.

Maybe this whole thing was an overreaction. He could admit that he did that sometimes when it came to people's safety. But the saying *Better safe than sorry* was his own personal mantra. Maybe it *was* someone who was ticked off Chloe had arrested them, and she was as trained and capable of handling it as anyone, but it could just as easily be a threat that pertained to last night's discovery. And that made everything more tenuous.

Either way, someone had laid a threat at her door. The real shock was, she hadn't really fought him on it. She'd gone inside, collected her things and her brother—maintaining a clear barrier between him and Ry.

Jack wasn't sure which one of them she didn't trust, truth be told. He was pretty sure she had a clear head when it came to her brother, but Jack also understood—even though his siblings tended to stay on the right side of the law—how easily someone you felt responsible for could blind you to the reality of a situation.

Jack pulled up to the main house, Chloe parking her car next to his truck. It was dark now, but the external house lights were on, along with a few internal.

Ry looked up at the house with wide eyes as he got out of Chloe's car. Jack understood the mind of an addict a little too well. He was likely adding up how many hits he could get for the different things he saw. Jack hoped for Chloe's sake that Ry could keep it together for this.

Ry didn't say anything. Chloe seemed pretty determined

to keep him and Jack from speaking at all, and Jack had no problem with that. He led them inside to where Mary was pacing the living room, Walker looking on disapprovingly from one of the armchairs.

"What happened?" Mary demanded. Not of Jack but of Chloe.

"Your brother overreacting?" She crouched and let Tiger go. The cat went all of three steps to lean against his leg.

"A mutilated snake was very purposefully strewn all over Chloe's porch sometime this evening," Jack said, trying to keep any and all inflection out of his voice.

Mary's expression pinched. "Then I have to agree with Jack about you guys coming here. That timing... When you've never had anything like that happen—and then all of the sudden, bones and snakes. I don't like it."

"Well, you've got us in your clutches now. The magical Hudson Ranch, where nothing bad happens," Chloe said, irreverently, of course.

Jack's scowl deepened, but he didn't have to defend his position. Mary did it for him, and Jack was well aware Mary's very pregnant belly helped soften the message, and Chloe's belligerence.

"We have an extensive security system. You won't even get one of those doorbell cameras at your cabin."

Chloe wrinkled her nose. "Those can't protect you. All they can do is potentially identify whoever might be engaging in criminal behavior in their view."

Jack narrowly resisted rolling his eyes.

"Well, we've got some rooms made up. Follow me and I'll show you where to put your things. Are you hungry? We'll get you all set up." Mary was ushering them out of the room and up the stairs before anyone had a chance to answer any of her questions.

Walker was standing now, frowning at the stairs after his wife. "I tried to tell her to relax and let someone else handle it."

"Yeah, how'd that work out for you?"

Walker grinned. "Yeah, well, I know she's exhausted, because she let me help make the beds."

"Are you sure you shouldn't take her to a hospital right now?"

"That's not funny. I tried."

Jack chuckled. If there was anything that gave him *some* level of comfort, it was the fact that his siblings had all ended up with people who tried to take care of them and ran into the same roadblocks he always did.

"This whole snake thing seems pretty personal. Meant to make her scared," Walker said, growing serious.

Jack nodded because he agreed with the assessment, but he didn't say anything else because he could also tell Walker was fishing.

"The thing is, stuff like that only scares you if you know why you're being threatened."

Jack tried not to tense. Failed. "First of all, she wasn't scared. Not nearly scared enough for the situation. Second, I've known Chloe a long time. She's one of my best deputies. She doesn't know anything, or she would have said."

"What about the brother?"

Jack's mouth firmed. He wasn't any fan of defending Ry Brink. The guy had given Chloe a lot of grief over the years, and Jack figured he'd earned all the negative talk aimed his way. But... "I'm not saying Ry couldn't be involved in *something*, but those bones were buried on the

Brink property a long, long time ago. Chloe *and* Ry would have been kids when it happened."

"Kids know things, too, Jack."

Unfortunately, Jack couldn't argue with that.

Chapter Six

Chloe didn't sleep well. When she caught snatches, she had dreams of skeletons and snakes. Her subconscious was *real* subtle.

The sun was only a faint glow in her window when she gave up and got out of bed. She'd check on Ry, go for a run and then figure out a way to sneak some coffee without having to sit down to a whole Hudson breakfast.

She considered tracking down her traitorous cat, but she had a feeling she knew exactly where Tiger would be this morning, and it was best if Chloe stayed away.

Satisfied with her plan, she got dressed in her running clothes, then quietly left the bedroom Mary had put her in last night. She knocked on the door next to hers—no answer. She eased the door open, but the room was empty. Dread curled in her stomach.

She thought she'd scared Ry enough into staying put, into not causing trouble, but when had that ever been the case?

She berated herself as she did her best to *silently* hurry down the stairs. She needed to make sure he'd left and wasn't wreaking havoc somewhere on Hudson property. Or sneaking around this house trying to sniff out some booze.

But when she reached the bottom of the stairs, she

breathed a small sigh of relief. Ry was there, creeping toward the front door. Maybe he'd slept and was only now considering his escape. She certainly hoped so.

"What the hell are you doing?" she hissed at him.

He jumped and whirled. Then his shoulders slumped in relief when his eyes landed on her. "I wasn't doing nothing," he whispered right back.

She didn't bother to correct his grammar like she might have ten years ago. Back then she'd been so sure she could change him, mold him, at least get him to graduate high school so he'd stop hanging out with their father and *his* no-good crew.

No such luck there. Now she just hoped she could keep him sober for however long she put up with the Hudsons trying to protect them from whatever was being threatened. Then go back to the hands-off life her therapist had suggested was best.

How on earth had she gotten twisted up in this very complicated situation? She should have known all those years ago, when her father had been adamant about transferring his assets to them before he'd been arrested, that having her name on the ownership of Brink land was only ever going to bring her trouble.

So much trouble.

She got close to Ry and waved her finger at him. "You promise me, *promise me*, you don't know what that snake thing was about?" She'd already had this conversation with him in the car last night, but he'd been a little drunk after finding her secret stash while she'd been out watching the sunset with Jack.

Because that was what a girl got for doing something she wanted to do.

But anyway, she wanted to make sure he'd still promise when he was sober.

"Nobody knew I was staying at your place, Chlo. Even if they did, they're gonna steer clear of a cop's house. Why would my friends want to mess with you?"

She believed him, mostly because for all the trouble she'd had with Ry before, it was nothing like this. Nothing that targeted her directly. He'd only ever asked her to get him *out* of trouble. Or for money. No petty dead-animal games with her brother's equally useless addict friends.

It really bugged her that the most reasonable explanation for the snakes was connecting it to the skeletal remains on the ranch. Bugged her because it meant she agreed with Jack, and it meant it would make sense for them to keep staying here.

But boy, was her brother the biggest liability.

"Morning."

Ry let out a little yelp of surprise, and Chloe reached for the gun she was not wearing, thank goodness. But when she turned to face the source of the voice—Jack, of course—she noted his raised eyebrow like he knew exactly what she'd been doing.

"Going somewhere?" he asked casually.

But there was nothing casual about the way he looked at Ry. Cop to criminal. Looking for signs that he'd done something wrong. Just like Chloe herself had done.

But when Jack did it, she had to fight the urge to stand between them. To defend her brother.

"A run," Chloe said, offering him her best sunny smile. "I was trying to convince Ry to go with me, but he's not much into exercise."

Jack nodded as if he believed her story. She knew he didn't.

"Chloe tells me you're good with animals," Jack said. Directly to Ry.

Ry stared at Jack, unblinking for a full minute. "Er, yes, sir."

Chloe wanted to laugh, even with her insides all twisted up. She wasn't sure she'd ever heard her brother call anyone *sir*, but Jack was the kind of guy who brought it out in people, she supposed.

"I've got a job for you, if you're wanting to avoid running."

"Uh." Ry looked at Chloe, clearly hoping for her to make an excuse for him.

"He'll take it," Chloe supplied instead. She didn't relish the idea of Jack and Ry hanging out, but she'd seen that look on her brother's face when she'd caught him trying to creep out of here. He'd been ready to go stir up some trouble, and the only thing that ever kept him out of trouble was work. Work with animals was even better. He *was* good with them. Much better than he was with people, that was for sure.

"Cash could always use a set of hands. I'll take you over." Jack tilted his head away from the front door and toward the back of the house. "Follow me."

"Uh. Okay," Ry said, clearly uncomfortable, but it was hard to argue with Jack when he was in Mr. Ruler of the World mode. Which was most of the time, she supposed.

Ry took a few hesitant steps forward before Jack began to lead him out of the room.

"You wait right here, Chloe," Jack said firmly, his back to her as he led Ry away. "We'll take that run together."

She scowled after his retreating form. She *hated* when he bossed her around. Well, in this kind of context, anyway. But since she was a guest in this house, she felt like she had to listen to him.

Which was really, really annoying.

JACK LED RY toward Cash's dog barns without saying anything. It was a bit early yet, even for the ranch, but Jack hadn't been able to sleep. He'd laid in his bed, staring at the ceiling, knowing Chloe was right above him. Talking himself out of going up there over and over again.

He felt terrible from lack of sleep, but he was damn proud of himself for having *some* restraint when it came to Chloe.

The morning was cool—a little overcast, so the dawn seemed to hang on longer than usual. Cash and Carlyle wouldn't be out at the barns just yet since it was so early, but it gave Jack a chance to have a one-on-one conversation with Ry Brink.

He studied the man. Slight and fidgety, but not angry. Uncertain and nervous, sure, but he didn't look like he was going to bolt or be defiant.

Jack didn't know what Chloe and Ry had been discussing this morning at the front door, but it definitely wasn't a *run*. A lecture about behavior, maybe, but Jack doubted Ry was up at the crack of dawn for *good* reasons.

Jack pointed to the dog barn in the distance. "You know about my brother Cash, right?"

"Sorta. He's got lots of dogs or something?" Ry looked around the barn like he was expecting them all to come running. "I do like dogs."

"He trains them, for all sorts of things. Carlyle Daniels

works for him helping train them, but they can always use another body. It's a lot of work, training them and making sure they're in good shape. If you like dogs, it's a good way to spend a day. And you can spend as many days as you like doing it, as long as you follow instructions."

Ry pulled a face at that. Jack sighed inwardly. He dealt with people all the time who didn't like to be told what to do—his family, people he pulled over, flat-out criminals—so he knew he had to lay this out in the simplest terms lest Ry be rebellious just for the sake of not following someone else's rules.

So he stopped, leaned on the fence and studied Ry with his most detached cop look. No emotion, no reaction. Just reason and sense. "I know you don't like cops—or me. And that's fine, I don't need you to."

Ry fidgeted, not meeting Jack's gaze.

"I know a lot of things about you, Ry. But first and foremost, I know this—your sister feels responsible for you. You mess this up, you mess her up."

Ry chewed on his bottom lip, looked around at the dusky dawn of morning across the ranch. "I know." Then he shrugged. "I don't do it on purpose. I don't like messing her up, but I can't seem to help it."

"Try. For as long as it takes to figure this out, give it your best shot. We can keep you busy. We can help in whatever ways you might need that don't include substance abuse. But I need to know you want to try."

Ry's frown was frustrated but not belligerent exactly. "I just like to have a little fun and get carried away sometimes."

"You're an addict, Ry. First step in helping your sister would be admitting that to yourself."

The frown turned into a scowl, with some pointed anger thrown in. "I didn't have anything to do with those bones, man."

"I don't think you did."

Ry looked up at him suspiciously. "Really?"

"It takes time for bodies to decompose, Ry. I can't imagine you were more than seven when those bodies were put in the ground. Even if they were newer, you don't strike me as mean enough to kill anybody."

"I'm not."

He did not say those words proudly. He said them almost as if he was ashamed of it. Jack couldn't say he liked that take on the matter. It gave him a different kind of worry— that Ry might *want* to be capable of murder.

But he could only handle one problem at a time. "Your dad, on the other hand…"

"It does sound like something my dad would do," Ry agreed. "I mean, I never heard about him killing anybody, but he sure liked to beat people up."

Jack knew this. He'd arrested Mark Brink for a domestic assault his first year working as a county deputy. But the girlfriend he'd beaten up had refused to press charges. And Jack never liked to think about what that might have meant for the childhood Chloe endured, even if her parents had divorced early on. But she'd bounced between the two— neither one upstanding, reliable or good parents, clearly.

"You ever see him get close?"

Ry sighed, not nervous or fidgety so much now. Bored. Craving a hit. Who knew. "The cops already asked me all about Dad. I don't have like some secret memory of him killing someone and burying them at the ranch, man. And there isn't anything in it for me if I protect him, so I ain't lying."

Jack nodded. Fair enough. And he'd told himself he'd stay out of it. He could hardly ask his siblings to do what he told them if he was investigating.

He had to let Bent County take care of it.

He squinted across the yard, saw Cash and Carlyle making their way from the main house. When they reached the fence where Jack and Ry were, Jack made introductions, even though Ry and Cash knew of each other.

Jack knew Cash and Carlyle could handle this, but still he hesitated leaving them with Ry. It felt a little bit too much like foisting his responsibilities off on someone else.

But he and Chloe had work, and this was the best-case scenario in keeping Ry out of trouble.

"You do as you're told, or I kick your ass. Got it?" Carlyle was saying to Ry after she'd explained their opening procedures with letting the dogs out.

Ry's eyes were wide, but he nodded. Carlyle flashed Jack a grin.

It did a lot to assuage his worries about leaving Ry here with them. Enough so that he headed back to the main house and Chloe. He wouldn't be surprised if she didn't wait for him, but he stopped by his bedroom and changed into clothes he could run in.

If it was a bluff, he'd call it. But when he returned to the living room, she was there—bending over, touching her toes, stretching out before her run, he assumed. And she was wearing skin-tight running gear, which did support her previous story. Yet he was having trouble thinking about anything but getting his hands on her.

He didn't know what it was about her that tested all that

hard-won control he'd always been so proud of. He'd been attracted to other women before, had *liked* other women before, but something about the package of Chloe Brink made him feel like an entirely different person than the one he'd so ruthlessly crafted over the years.

She stopped stretching, looked over her shoulder at him. She didn't say anything, didn't voice her concerns, but he saw them in her eyes.

"Carlyle's in charge of keeping him in line," he said. "I think he's afraid of her."

Her mouth quirked. "Well, that does ease my concerns about going to work later. Carlyle *can* handle him. For a while, anyway."

"He'll be okay."

Chloe shrugged. "Maybe. Maybe not. But I can't twist my life around him. Learned that one the hard way." She blew out a breath. "Thought my cat would be trailing after you, per usual."

"Tiger found someone he likes better than even me." When she raised an eyebrow, he couldn't stop himself from smiling. "Izzy."

Chloe smiled at that too, as he'd been hoping she would. "Well, he's in good hands, then."

"So, run?"

Her smile died and she sighed. "You hate running, Jack."

"I don't hate it."

"You *hate* it, and I think your family would find it a little weird you're doing something you hate with me at the butt crack of dawn. I don't need a bodyguard."

Which was probably true, and maybe he should just let this go. But he didn't. "I didn't realize you were an expert on the layout of the Hudson Ranch."

She rolled her eyes. "Jack."

"Chloe."

Something in her expression hardened. "I think you're supposed to call me Deputy Brink here."

He didn't know what this was about, but he could admit that something about being *here* made him a whole lot less interested in ignoring any tension there was between them. "Do you want to have a fight about it?"

She huffed out a breath. "No."

"Then let's go run."

"Fine," she muttered.

He led her outside, pointed to the fence line. "We can follow this out toward the highway, then turn back. Should be about two and a half miles."

"I usually do five."

Jack tried not to pull a face. "We can do it twice, then." What a waste of time.

But then she laughed and slapped him gently in the chest. "Messing with you. One round is fine. Think you can beat me?"

"My legs are longer."

"Is that a yes?" she returned, eyebrows raised.

But he only shrugged. She shook her head. "All right, buddy. Ready, set, go." Then she took off. Too fast to start a two-and-a-half-mile run. Or so he thought in the beginning. He assumed he'd catch up to her, but she always maintained a distance. It got slimmer the longer they ran, but even when he began to pour it on, she kept ahead of him.

When the house came back into view, he ran as hard as he could manage. He made it close, but she still beat him. And they both ended in the front yard, bent over hands on their knees, panting.

And laughing. He didn't know why she was laughing. Maybe because she'd won. He was laughing because it was ridiculous, when he very rarely got prodded into the ridiculous. He was laughing because it didn't seem to matter what they did or why—just being around her lifted all those weights on his shoulders he'd thought were permanent.

The way she laughed, smiled, enjoyed the smallest things.

"You're going to have to run with me all the time now," she said, wiping her forehead with her forearm. "Beating you is my best time in a while."

All the time. He tried not to think about it, because their jobs made it impossible, but he wondered if she knew how little he'd mind *all the time.* Forever.

When she looked over at him, gave him a little chest pat he figured was supposed to be a friendly, *good game*–type gesture, he couldn't help himself. He held her by the wrist, pulled her in.

She didn't resist, but she did look up at him warily. "Anyone could see us, Jack."

"Yeah." But he didn't move, and neither did she.

Chapter Seven

Chloe did not understand what was happening between them. For an entire *year*, the lines had been very clear, and both of them had been dedicated to keeping it that way.

But the past few days were getting all muddled, blurry, when it was the last thing that should be happening, what with skeletal remains and mutilated snakes and her own damn family. It was turning her soft.

Because she should have pushed him away, but she let him kiss her here. In broad daylight. In front of the Hudson house, which housed like a hundred people. People who would have questions, who would tell other people, who would erase all the lines they'd carefully drawn.

And still she drowned in the kiss. They weren't supposed to *do* this, but she couldn't stop herself because he kissed her with a gentleness that undid all her paltry walls. These were the ones that really got to her. He didn't pull this out often. Usually, there wasn't time for soft, leisurely. But his hands were on her face, his grip gentle as the kiss spun out into something that reached deeper than anything else ever had, until she felt like gravity simply ceased to exist.

He eased back, his dark eyes studying her face, his mouth still just a breath from hers. She wasn't quite sure how, after a year of sneaking around, something could change, but something had.

Maybe this place was magic. *Or a curse.*

She had to shake her head to get both ridiculous thoughts out. Step away from him to find some anchor in this storm. "We have to get to work." Her voice shook.

"Yeah." His voice didn't, but his exhale did.

Well, at least there was that.

She should break it off. Stop this right now. Before it got more complicated.

It was already way too complicated.

But she walked back into his home, shoulder to shoulder to him, and didn't say a word. They went their separate ways in the house, and she ran through the shower upstairs, got dressed for work and then ignored Mary's insisting she eat something. She knew Jack expected to drive her over to her cabin and drop her off at her cruiser, but she needed some space.

She didn't even get halfway to her car before she heard him call her name. She turned. He'd also showered, changed into work clothes. He looked put together as always, in his perfectly pressed khakis and Sunrise Sheriff's Department polo.

His expression was very grim, which wasn't all that unusual for work, but there was something about him that had her tensing.

"We have to get to the hospital," he said, striding toward his cruiser.

"The hospital. Why?"

"Suzanne just called me," he said, referring to the Sunrise administrative assistant. "Kinsey was at your place when—"

"You had someone watch my cabin overnight?" she demanded, surprised by this brand-new information, which he had neither shared with her nor asked permission to *do*.

"No, I had someone drive by a few times overnight and—"

"Without telling me?"

"Yeah, without telling you. Now, would you let me finish?" He jerked open the driver's-side door. "Kinsey was shot at. Suzanne says it was just a graze, but he's at the hospital getting it looked at, and we need to go down there and get his story."

Chloe's heart slammed against her chest, enough to get over the frustration with Jack doing all that without telling her. She hopped into the passenger seat. "You sure he's okay? Should I call Julie?" Steve's wife would no doubt be worried sick.

Steve Kinsey had been with Sunrise since its inception, moving with Jack over from Bent County. He was in his late forties and had three teenagers at home, who he liked to bemoan even though he did everything he could to take time off to make all their many birthdays, holidays and sporting events.

"He called Julie himself. He's fine," Jack said, pulling out of the Hudson Ranch and onto the main highway, which would take them into Hardy and to the hospital.

But his hands were so tight on the wheel that his knuckles were white. Back to a perfectly capable outer shell and nothing inside but ticking time bombs.

Chloe blew out a slow breath, trying to focus on the important things. Steve had been shot. At her cabin? "Was someone trying to break in?"

"Suzanne didn't have the details. We'll get them from him ourselves."

They drove for a while in silence. Sometimes she wished

she couldn't read him so easily. She tried—so hard—to keep her mouth shut. To let him deal with his stuff without trying to offer some kind of comfort.

This was work. This was that line they had *both* agreed on. And it was a line that had worked for a *year*.

But as they approached the hospital, she couldn't keep it in any longer. "It could have been anything, Jack. Not just the thing you asked him to do. That's the job."

"But it wasn't anything, was it?" Jack pulled the cruiser in front of the hospital, and they got out at the same time.

Jack took the lead, a sheriff down to the bone as he talked to the front desk and a nurse, before they were finally led into a room.

Steve sat on an exam table and even smiled at them—if ruefully—when they entered.

"I'm fine, boss. Just grazed me." He wiggled his bandaged arm. "Not even keeping me." He nodded at Chloe, then looked back at Jack. "I didn't see anything, though, that's the kicker."

"As long as you're okay, that doesn't matter."

Steve clearly didn't agree, but he didn't argue with the sheriff. He launched into an explanation. "I was driving by Brink's house on my way back to the station. Thought *maybe* I saw a light. Figured she'd just left one on, but since there'd been some trouble, I got out to check it out."

"You radioed that in?"

Steve nodded. "I parked in the driveway, turned the flashlight on and started to walk toward the side of the house. Told myself I was overreacting—but then, out of nowhere, I just heard *pop*. And felt it." He gestured at the bandage. "That was it, though. Must have run off. If they'd wanted real trouble, they would have *really* shot me. Would have been easy pickings," he said disgustedly.

Chloe felt sick at the thought.

"I called it in to Suzanne. I was ready to go check out the backyard, but Suzanne's fussing about ambulances and blah, blah, blah. I think Bent County is out there looking at it now."

"Bent County? But it's our jurisdiction," Chloe said.

Steve's expression was unreadable. "Sort of."

"What does 'sort of' mean?" Chloe demanded as Steve's gaze moved to Jack. "Jack, what does that mean?"

If Steve thought it was weird that she'd used his first name instead of *Sheriff*, he didn't act like it.

"I reported the snake to Bent County."

She didn't know exactly why that made her so angry except that he was…taking over while keeping her out of it. Something that involved *her* ranch, *her* brother, *her* house, her *life*. "I live in Sunrise."

"Yes, and I happen to think all of this connects to what was found on the ranch. And that's Bent County's case. Besides, it's a conflict of interest for Sunrise to investigate."

"That's *if* it has something to do with *me*. And I wasn't home. Either time. Maybe they thought I would be, should be, but it seems strange that if this was about *me*, they wouldn't make sure they knew exactly where I was."

"Unless they didn't want you there," Steve suggested. "Seems to me, creeping around your cabin is looking for something. Maybe they were looking for your brother."

Chloe didn't glare at Steve. She didn't even look at him. She kept her ire focused on Jack. Even if none of this was his fault, either, he was an easier target.

But his eyebrows were drawn together as though he was

thinking. "Maybe it's not *you*. Not Ry. Maybe they *wanted* you out of the way. Maybe there's something *in* the cabin they want."

"What could I have in the ca…" She trailed off, a horrible thought occurring to her. "Some of my father's things. I have them in my garage."

JACK DROVE TO Chloe's cabin. She said nothing, and he didn't know what to say either, so the ride was in absolute silence. Seeing Steve had eased some of the tension about the situation—he really was fine and thinking clearly, but Jack still didn't like any of his deputies being hurt on the job.

But it *was* the job. And he had to focus on the next step of it: trying to figure out why someone suddenly had Chloe—or Ry, or her cabin—in their sights.

He pulled his truck into the driveway. Jack frowned at the fact that there wasn't anyone here. "I should call someone at County."

Chloe shook her head, already getting out of the truck. "If there was something to say, they'd be here or they'd have called me."

Jack sighed and followed her. She went right for the garage, that determined focus stamped into the expression on her face.

"He did all this stuff before he got arrested," she was saying, opening the garage, striding toward a bunch of boxes. "Wanted us to spend time on the ranch with him. Told us it was our *legacy*."

She started moving boxes, and Jack wanted to help, but he didn't know what she was looking for, and it seemed like maybe she just had to do this herself.

"He tells me he wants us on the deed. I've done all right for myself, if being a government patsy is all right. But he's worried about Ry. Wants Ry to run it, even though it's not profitable—but hey, it's a house. It's *something*, I figured." She tossed a tub out of the way. "Used all my guilt, all my worry about Ry to get my name on there too." She shook her head, clearly disgusted with herself.

"My first year at Sunrise. I know I was green, but I also knew *him*. I should have seen it for what it was. A criminal who knew his time was up. He tells me he's getting rid of stuff so he can be 'free' and all this other nonsense. Asks me if I want some family heirlooms. I should have said no. I *know* I should have said no, but I—"

"Nothing wrong with wanting family heirlooms, Chloe."

"Oh, come on, Jack. I know who my family is. Criminals begetting criminals. Sure, maybe I hoped somewhere along the line, the Brinks had this ranch because *someone* wasn't totally worthless. Maybe there was some immature fantasy about inheriting a sense of right and wrong from *someone*, but I know better. I should have known better."

She finally stopped moving things, her breath coming in pants from the physical exertion. There was an old antique-looking chest pressed back in the corner of the garage.

She glared at it. "I never looked through it. He used to do this thing. I couldn't quite believe it *wasn't* heirlooms, but I knew. I knew it was just the usual way he liked to mess with me."

"And how was that?"

She shrugged jerkily. "Once my parents really split, he was in and out of our lives. Sometimes he'd come around and Mom was tired of us, and we'd have to go spend a week or two at the ranch with him. He'd always have presents. For me. But they were just…joke gifts."

Jack doubted he'd agree with the word *joke*, but he didn't press. He had to bite the inside of his cheek to keep his mouth shut, but he did it.

"I should have looked through it and gotten rid of it." She swallowed, clearly emotional about the whole thing. "I was a coward."

"You're human, Chloe."

She didn't look at him, just kept staring at the chest.

And this was work. They weren't Chloe and Jack here. He was the sheriff. She was a deputy. There was a case to untangle. One they were both way too close to. He should call in Bent County for this, but…

She needed to handle this first step herself. She undid the latch, but paused before she lifted the lid and took a deep breath. She looked up at him.

"Whatever this is, Jack, I need you to keep in mind that if those remains are your parents, the chances my family had *nothing* to do with it are slim to none."

He knew she was right. That all the ways this was twisting was likely leading to a very clear place. Maybe that should matter to him, but with her staring at him like that, all emotionally wounded, it just didn't.

"Maybe."

She shook her head, and her eyes were a little shiny, enough to make his heart twist. When she spoke, though, she was firm.

"Not maybe. Basic reason."

"You're not your family, Chloe." He wished he could make her believe that. Wished there were some magical words he could find to erase all that pain for her.

"But they're mine all the same," she muttered, then lifted the lid.

She jumped back with a little shriek he'd never once heard come out of her. He moved, with half a thought to protect her from whatever was inside, but the scene in the chest had him recoiling as well.

Dolls. A lot of them. Mutilated and smeared in what Jack could only assume had been blood.

Chapter Eight

Chloe should not have been surprised. She certainly shouldn't have shrieked. Another joke gift. She should have known— she *had* known, but she'd wanted to live in hope that some-where along the line, the name Brink hadn't been garbage. As long as this chest had remained closed, she could pre-tend there were nice family heirlooms inside. Artifacts of a family line that wasn't just waste.

She should have sucked it up, been a realist and dealt with this a million years ago. Because *now* she had to deal with it in front of Jack. Served her right, she guessed.

"It was a dumb thought," she managed to say, though her voice was rough. She moved forward, tried to keep her arms from shaking and failed as she flipped the lid closed. "No one's after this. Just his usual stunts. Probably laughed himself all the way to jail on this one."

Jack took her by the arm, started steering her out of the garage. Away from the chest, thank God. What was she going to do now? She needed to haul it out of here. She needed…

"You go on inside," Jack said. His voice was gentle, but *cop* gentle. Devoid of real emotion. Just getting the job done. "I'm going to call in Bent County. I'll put on gloves and look through it while we wait for Hart or Delaney-Carson to get here."

Panic spurted through her. No one needed to see this. No one needed to start sorting through all the gross, messed-up pointlessness of a childhood with Mark Brink as a father.

Worse than that, the idea of Jack sorting through all those horrible, gruesome dolls when she knew something worse might be lurking.

Dear old Dad had made sure to be clear that it could always, *always* be worse.

She didn't pull out of Jack's grasp, but she did move in front of him and plant her feet so he couldn't keep ushering her out. "Don't do that, Jack. Not alone. Not…" She couldn't articulate how little she wanted Jack wading through this. "He did this kind of thing. It's not—"

"Someone was sneaking around your place, willing to shoot at an officer. There are dead bodies buried on a ranch with your name on the deed. A mutilated snake was purposefully left on your porch. All in the span of forty-eight hours. We need to look into everything. No matter how off the wall it feels. No matter how little you want to."

"You think he did it. Murdered your parents. Buried them on his ranch. You think this is a clue, but—"

"*You* think he did it, Chloe," Jack said gently, and the grasp on her arm softened, his palm sliding down to her hand. He covered it with his, squeezed. "I don't know what to think. So we'll take it a step at a time. I don't want you seeing this. I'll go through it. You go inside."

She swallowed the lump in her throat that just kept growing. "There could be worse in there. I don't want *you* going through it. What if there's something…"

"Something?"

"He's an abusive, violet criminal. Those dolls could be just a scare tactic he thought was funny, or they could be hiding something worse."

Jack studied her face, something grim and…looking a lot like fury seeming to darken his gaze. Emotionless cop gone, just like that. "Were the joke gifts he gave you when you were a kid *usually* hiding something worse?"

She held herself very still, purposefully blocking out old memories she didn't want to show on her face. Her father's had never stuck around long. She liked to pretend he hadn't been there at all.

But he'd done damage in what little spaces he'd had. It didn't take a *lot* of bad experiences to know he was capable of awful things. Only one, and the threat of a repeat.

She did not want Jack knowing that, but she couldn't seem to come up with a lie to get that protective look off his face. Like he could go back in time and make it all right.

"It doesn't matter," she managed.

"Chl—"

"I said, it doesn't matter, and it doesn't. This isn't about… It was a mistake to think this is connected. It's a mistake to start digging into…" But she couldn't finish that sentence because if her father was responsible for the dead bodies on the Brink Ranch—and God knew that was looking more and more likely—everything he'd done back then would be examined under a microscope to determine motive, means and opportunity.

She wanted to throw up.

"What happened to you when you were a kid isn't—"

She couldn't take his pity. She wouldn't. "I've had therapy, Jack. I've dealt with my garbage bin of a childhood. I don't need you and your perfect one psychoanalyzing me."

She sucked in a breath, immediately regretting everything she'd just said. She could have punched herself for how insensitive it was. Sure, he'd had a great childhood— but then, he'd also spent every second of his adulthood stepping into his missing parents' shoes. "I'm sorry."

He shook his head like it didn't matter. But it did. This all mattered, and she *hated* it.

She moved her hand so she was grasping his instead of the other way around. She looked into those dark, fathomless eyes, and she didn't care if she was begging. She just needed this to not explode on her. "Please. I wouldn't ask this of you if it didn't matter. Please. Don't." She wouldn't cry. "Let the detectives handle it. With the right gear, the right warning." She *wouldn't* cry. Not in front of Jack—her *boss*. Because that's what he was right now.

Not the guy who'd kissed her this morning like she was special. It didn't do any good to think about that completely separate moment.

"Okay." His free arm came around her, pulled her close. Even though they both wore their uniforms. Their gun belts. Their radios. He shouldn't do this. She shouldn't let him.

But she didn't pull away, because she was shaking, and if he held her, maybe she could find some anchor in the midst of all this mess.

JACK COULDN'T CONVINCE Chloe to go inside, but he did get her to sit down on the stoop of her cabin porch—where he'd just cleaned up snake remains yesterday.

Only forty-eight hours. No, he didn't like this, or that it pointed to something more *current* happening around a very old potential murder.

He glanced back at her. She'd been startled by the snake,

but it hadn't really affected her. This? It had shaken her. He'd never seen her quite so affected by *anything*, not that he couldn't blame her for it. The dolls were creepy enough on their own—add the fact that it was clearly and purposefully done to mess with her by her own father…

Jack supposed it was a good thing Mark Brink was in prison over a thousand miles away, because the way all this information settled inside him was testing his usually impeccable control.

As it was, he focused on the present. He didn't sit next to her on the stoop. It seemed to agitate her more. So he stood just out of reach, waiting for Bent County to arrive.

When they did, Jack handled everything. He wasn't sure that was what she wanted, and he knew he could be overbearing—his siblings made sure he knew. He didn't mind it when it came to them, but it bothered him with Chloe.

She had a say too, but this was… Like anything else, he couldn't protect her from *everything*. But he would protect her from what he could.

Besides, he was the sheriff.

So he instructed the deputies to take the chest away and search it with the utmost caution and keep everything as potential evidence for the time being. When the detectives arrived, Jack explained the situation, and they did what they were supposed to do.

Hart separated Jack from Chloe and asked *him* questions about what had happened while Laurel no doubt did the same with Chloe. Jack didn't like it, but he understood they were doing their job. A job complicated by the fact that the people involved were also cops.

Jack could see Laurel and Chloe on the porch, but Hart

had pulled him out by his cruiser close to the street, so he had no idea what Laurel was asking or how Chloe was answering. But he had to focus on the questioning *he* was part of.

He explained what had led them to look at the chest, what he'd seen, what Chloe had said about it. Hart noted down his answers, and once he was satisfied, he switched gears to all their other issues.

"Since Mark Brink would have lived on the land at the time of your parents' disappearance, we've already been looking into him," Hart explained, "in regards to the remains. Just to get an idea of the players if the ID is positive. We called the correctional facility in Texas, and they got back to us this morning."

Jack could tell by the way Hart said it that the news wasn't going to be good.

"He got out on parole last week."

Jack swore.

"So far he's cooperated with his parole officer. It'd be quite the feat for him to get up here, wait around until the cabin was empty, do all that with the mutilated snake and then get back for his check-in."

"A feat, but not impossible."

"No, not impossible," Hart agreed. "We're arranging to have an interview with him. It might be another day or two. Lots of red tape to wade through."

"Isn't there always," Jack muttered. He really had no idea what to do with this information. It was such a strange thing, to have all these answers visible but out of reach. There was still the off chance those remains weren't even his parents'—though he didn't hold out any hope for that.

Maybe he hadn't given up on hope, on answers, but he

hadn't thought they'd land on his doorstep one random day with Chloe in tow. Surrounded by all these seemingly disparate events.

"Speaking of red tape," Hart continued. "Zeke got us hooked up with a forensic anthropologist. She got here this morning. We've got to get through some paperwork to make sure everything goes smoothly from a legal standpoint, but she should be able to get to work tomorrow. Once she can examine the remains, she'll have an ETA on identification. We'll keep moving forward with the investigation, but it's going to take time to narrow down time frames."

Jack nodded stiffly.

"We're sorry we don't have more clear-cut answers for you just yet, but we're working on it."

"Luckily, I know how it all works."

"Not sure how lucky that is."

Jack tried to force a smile but knew he didn't manage. He glanced back at the porch, where Laurel and Chloe were still talking. Chloe had definitely put her cop mask back on. She didn't look upset or rattled.

But it was lurking underneath. How could it not?

"Look, I know Brink is one of your deputies," Hart said, lowering his voice to almost a whisper even though Chloe wouldn't be able to hear them from this distance. "But this is bound to get messy. It might be better if you kept some distance. I'm not sure her and Ry Brink being in the Hudson Ranch-Hudson Sibling Solutions circle is the best move here."

Jack let Hart have his say, and he didn't bother to argue or defend himself. He just said his response in the simplest terms there were. "It's the only move here."

Because he'd be damned if he was going to keep his

distance from Chloe when she might be in some kind of danger. He walked away from Hart, not about to wait for the man's permission.

He was a sheriff. Head of the Hudson clan. And damn if he was going to be scared of *messy* when Chloe might have to pay the cost of that fear.

Laurel moved away from Chloe before Jack reached the porch, and she nodded at him. "I'll keep you updated on what we find. We'll treat it like a joint Sunrise-Bent County venture for as long as that makes sense. Unless you want to be kept out of this part too?"

Jack shook his head. "I want to know everything about that chest."

Laurel didn't say anything, but she didn't hide the fact she was studying him either. Then she shrugged and walked over to Hart, and the two took their leave.

Chloe approached Jack, chin up, eyes fierce and a little bright. He could already tell there was a storm brewing deep underneath.

"Whatever you're about to say, don't," he said. His temper was already on edge due to a million things, and he didn't need whatever she was gearing herself up to say to send him over.

"Why not?" she replied.

"Because I can tell it's going to tick me off."

She shook her head. "It's better if we don't stay with you, Jack."

"Better for who?" he returned, just barely holding on to that thread of calm.

"Everyone involved," Chloe said, and her expression was set, her voice firm, but there was something hiding underneath that cop mask. "Certainly better for you guys getting the answers you deserve."

"Did Laurel put that in your head, or is it your own wrongheaded thinking?"

She scowled at him, but he wasn't about to relent.

"Jack—"

"You and Ry are guests of the Hudson Ranch until we have some answers on the threats against you. I don't care what anyone, including you, has to say about it. That's what's happening."

"There aren't any threats against me. That snake *could* have been for Ry. Whatever my dad was pulling with those dolls happened *six* years ago. I'm not in any danger."

"I'm glad you feel that way. I don't."

"And Jack Hudson's feelings trump all else?" she demanded, but the heat wasn't there. She was just trying to pick a fight.

He was feeling a bit like letting her, but he took a deep breath. Reminded himself that whatever that chest of dolls was or wasn't, it had hurt her. Deeply enough that he'd seen all her usual masks fall.

He didn't want to add to that hurt. He never wanted to be even a contributing factor to her hurt.

But he had been. Not like this. Not deep, childhood wounds. But the nature of everything they'd been for the past year had not always been easy, and he knew…no matter how careful he tried to be, that she'd been hurt by the secret nature of what they did together outside of work.

And he knew she still believed it was for all the reasons *she* saw when that wasn't it at all. Maybe he'd have liked her to have given him more credit, to admit to herself that wasn't *him*, but… That wasn't very fair of him. He saw it more and more clearly as time went on, as little things about the way she'd grown up came out.

How she trusted anyone or anything, saw the good in anyone, *laughed* with people was beyond him. He was in *awe* of her.

Even as she kept going, determined to have that fight he couldn't muster up the anger for.

"Did it ever occur to you that I can handle me? And I can handle Ry? And I can handle *this*?" she demanded, working up to mad so she didn't have to be sad, scared, hurt. *Clearly.*

It killed him how easy it was to see through it, even as she kept on.

"Did it ever occur to you that I don't need this Jack Hudson, king of the world, 'I'll protect everyone and everything the sun touches just because I slept with you'?"

It was the strangest out-of-body thing. To watch her get mad as hell, to watch her gear it toward him, and not find himself being reactive at all. No, it was like all those walls he'd carefully erected for so long just crumbled to dust. Not even dramatically. Just slowly and silently to ash that flew away on the breeze.

"Well?" she demanded, her cheeks pink with anger, her hands on her hips and everything about her combative.

But he saw that little kernel of vulnerability she was trying so hard to protect, and for the first time in his life, he found himself handing over his own without even thinking about it.

"Did it ever occur to you that I'm in love with you?"

Chapter Nine

Chloe knew what he'd just said. She'd heard it. He'd sounded out that word, spoken it. Right here.

But she couldn't *understand* it. She couldn't put together the *knowledge* with the reality of Jack Hudson standing there saying...

No. *No.* He was...

No.

This was the weirdest time to tell someone they...

No, he was just trying to trick her. To get what he wanted. Which was protecting everyone and everything. And yeah, it wasn't like he *hated* her, but it was... It was...?

Why was her heart doing this terrible, hopeful dance in her chest? She knew better. She knew so much better. Chloe didn't trust love. How could she?

"Jack..." She tried to say more, but her throat was so tight, she couldn't seem to get words out. And he was standing in her yard, looking so good and strong and perfect.

God knew she wasn't meant for *that*.

"I think somewhere deep down, you have to know that. You know me, Chloe. Why else would I break any rule?"

She couldn't come up with an answer for that, and she tried. She tried so hard.

"So yeah, I have some issues when it comes to protecting people. I wonder why," he said, so dryly she might have laughed in another context.

But he'd said he *loved* her, and there was absolutely nothing funny about this horror show.

It had to be horror coursing through her. What else could it be?

"I'm overbearing. I think I'm right pretty much all the time." He took a few steps forward, and she had no choice but to scramble back. Away. Until he stopped moving toward her.

He couldn't touch her right now. She'd…she'd crumble.

"But I don't cross lines," he continued. "I don't break rules. I don't do *gray area*. Except when it comes to you. And if that was about fun or sex or whatever, I would have resisted. I would have put a stop to it. I would not have engaged in this whole thing for a *year*."

"Secretly," Chloe whispered, because it was the only thing she had to hold on to right now. The last line of defense against whatever he was doing to her.

"Yes, secretly. Because no matter how or when this comes out, I know how it shakes down, Chloe. I know how people will treat you. How they'll treat me. There will be whispers for sure, at a minimum."

She couldn't breathe. He'd *thought* about an "after everyone found out"? He'd considered the *consequences*? When all she'd ever done was…be sure he wouldn't want them without thinking what they might be.

"I can take it. At worst, I suffer a few comments and lose a few votes during my next sheriff election, but I still win. I won't be a party to having people question you, though. Your character or anything else. I know that most of our department won't have a problem with this, but there's a wider world, and I won't listen to people at Bent County pretend to know who you are or what you stand for because of your relationship with me. No number of speeches or interventions or *loving you* can change what people will say when I'm not there to stop it, and I never want you to have to deal with that."

She could only stare at him. All this time… All this *time*, and she'd been so sure she understood what they were doing. She'd known part of it was about work, about not breaking his precious rules, but she hadn't thought about…

And he had. What it would really look like if people knew about them. He'd thought it through. And he cared, deeply, that it would affect *her*.

She wanted so badly to protect her heart. Everyone who'd ever had it had bashed it into a million pieces.

But Jack laid out the reality of their situation, and she could see it. He laid it out and she *knew* him.

Of course the secrecy was about protecting *her*. *Of course* it wasn't superficial, about her family reputation—poor Jack didn't have an ounce of superficial in him.

Which only left one thing.

"Jack, I can't…"

"You don't have to do anything, Chloe. That's not why I said it. I said it so you'd understand. So you'd stop fighting me on this because you think… I don't know. That it doesn't matter to me? I need you to be careful. I need you to *care* that something dangerous is going on, one way or another."

This time when he moved for her, she let him. Let him take her hands in his. Let him look at her like…

Like he loved her. Because Jack Hudson, somehow and very inexplicably, was in love with her. And Jack didn't lie, except maybe sometimes to himself. But this wasn't that.

"I care that you are safe, Chloe. That you are...*happy* isn't the right word, but that you're okay. I have no feelings one way or another on your brother. I know you love him. I know how hard and complicated that is for you, and I respect it. And because I love *you*, I'm going to honor it. For as long as it takes, I need to protect you and Ry. And I need you to let me. That's all I need from you right now."

The fact that he was including Ry, that he understood just how complicated and frustrating her love for her brother was, made the tears she'd so desperately been battling all afternoon fall over.

I need you to let me. She'd give him so much—anything, really. He had to know it. "You're not playing fair," she managed to say, even as tears trailed down her cheeks.

He reached out and wiped them away. "I might play by the rules, but that doesn't mean I have to play fair."

She managed a watery laugh, but it died quickly because maybe she could believe he loved her. Maybe she would give him that thing he needed—the chance to protect her and Ry. But he was ignoring something very important.

"You have to look at the very real possibility that my father killed or had something to do with the murder of your parents. You can't just brush it away. Because when this is all figured out, it's going to matter. You have to really think about what that's going to be like."

Jack nodded. "I have."

"But—"

"No. No buts. I understand. If it's true, if we finally have the answers my family has wanted for seventeen years, it'll be a relief. But it won't bring them back, and it won't change anything. Not really."

"I'll be a reminder."

"No. You're not an extension of your father, Chloe. Any more than you're an extension of your mother or Ry. You're you, and I love you."

He said it so earnestly, holding her hands, looking at her tearstained face. Coming up with an answer for every one of her arguments. Taking away all the excuses she'd held herself up on for the past year.

It was scary—the scariest thing, really, because this had the potential to go so very wrong. But when he looked at her like that, she wanted to be someone else, just for a little bit. Someone who could just enjoy the fact that the man she'd been pining after for far too long had feelings for her too.

No, not just feelings. *Loved* her.

"You know, I've been in love with you for longer," she managed to say, not quite sounding like her usual self, but closer. More in charge.

His mouth quirked up at one side. "Is it a contest?"

She nodded emphatically. "Absolutely."

"Okay, how about this?" He pulled her close, brought his mouth next to hers. "I'll love you best," he murmured. Then sealed that promise with a kiss.

JACK HUDSON WAS a planner. He had emergency backup plans to the emergency backup plans. And yet it had never served him. He'd focused for the past seventeen years on wielding more and more control, and still…he'd never actually gotten it.

Grant had gone to war. Palmer and Anna had gone to the rodeo. Cash had gotten his high school girlfriend pregnant at sixteen. Not exactly a great parental track record to his way of thinking, certainly not if he compared himself to what his parents might have been able to do.

Then, over the past two years, Grant had been hurt on Dahlia's case; Palmer had been hurt and Louisa had been kidnapped; Anna had gotten pregnant, almost burned alive; and Mary had been kidnapped by a madman. And that didn't even get into everything that had happened with Cash when his ex-wife had tried to frame him for murder.

And every time something terrible had happened, Jack had tried to hold on tighter and tighter only to be reminded it never really mattered.

Bad things happened.

Loving Chloe wasn't a bad thing, but it was a complicated thing, and for all the ways he planned for twists and turns of fate—the inevitable *bad*—he had not ever once come up with a plan for what happened on the other side of *I'm in love with you.*

They drove to the station in silence, the weight of it sitting there between them. Because now they had to go into work.

Maybe next time he could plan love confessions around their work schedule.

"You should have let me drive my own cruiser," she muttered as he pulled up to the building that housed the Sunrise Sheriff's Department.

"Everyone will understand why I want you riding two-man right now. In fact, they'll probably be surprised I'm not making you take some leave."

She glared at him. "I'll take leave over *your* dead body."

"I know, that's why I'm not going to make you." He'd certainly considered it, but he wasn't about to tell her that.

She grunted and pushed out of the car, and he realized this wasn't so much her real frustration as it was her trying to build that wall back. So they could walk into their place of work and not have what they'd just laid out between each other broadcast to the world.

Jack had long ago given up on the world being fair. He never expected it. But it struck him in a way it hadn't in a long time what a bad hand they'd been dealt with this.

Still, he let Chloe blaze her way in first, and he took his time following. When he walked into the office, Suzanne immediately got to her feet. "Sheriff, is it true?"

For a second, Jack was distracted enough to think she was talking about everything that had just happened with Chloe. Which was ridiculous. The look on Suzanne's face was clear. Anguish.

Suzanne Smithfield, Sunrise's administrative assistant, had known both his parents. Well, everyone in town had. People loved to tell him stories about how one of his parents had helped them out of a bad situation. But Suzanne had been close personal friends with them. She'd gone to school with his dad, and his mother had babysat Suzanne's kids sometimes.

He managed a reassuring smile for Suzanne. "We don't have ID confirmation yet. It's probably going to take a while. Don't let the gossip mill upset you."

Suzanne sighed heavily. "The news hasn't made its way through town yet, but it will. And soon enough."

Jack nodded. "That's all right. I'll handle it."

"You handle too much, Sheriff."

"So they say."

She leaned in close. "All this stuff with Chloe's cabin… Is it related?"

Most people asking that question would put his back up, but he knew Suzanne cared about each and every Sunrise deputy like one of her own kids. She was worried about

Chloe, nothing else. "We don't know yet, but Deputy Brink and her brother are going to be staying out at the ranch until we get it sorted. I also want her riding two-man for the time being, so keep an eye out if she tries to dance around that."

Suzanne nodded. "Good. That's good." Then she nodded to his office. "Messages are on your desk."

Jack nodded, then focused on being Sheriff Jack Hudson and nothing else. He returned messages, worked on some paperwork, did what needed to be done. And if he occasionally took a walk around the office to get more coffee than necessary to check on Chloe, well...

Who knew that was what he was doing besides himself?

But she had calls to respond to and work, too, so their paths didn't cross, and that was fine. Great, even. Best all the way around.

If it settled in him like frustration, he was just going to have to get used to that.

Toward the end of the day, he got a call from Bent County. When he heard Hart on the other end, Jack doubted they had good news coming.

"We haven't got a hold of Mark Brink yet, but we did get a report he was spotted in Denver. Morning after the remains were found."

Denver. Pretty much halfway between Texas and them. "Going to ask around and see if anyone saw him here?"

"Already got a deputy on it. Laurel's also going to head out to the ranch and question Ry again."

"Why?"

"That's a pretty quick turnaround, Jack. Being in Denver the morning after a middle-of-the-night discovery? If it's connected, he had warning."

Jack closed his eyes and tried not to groan. He wanted to

argue with Hart, but how could he? If he was in charge of the investigation, he'd been drilling Ry for information too.

"Phone records?" Jack asked, though it squeezed his heart to do it. Chloe was a realist when it came to her brother, but that didn't mean she was going to be okay with any of this.

"Working on a search warrant, but Laurel's going to see if he'll hand it over of his own free will. Ry doesn't strike me as a hardened criminal despite his rap sheet, but I don't know what kind of relationship he has with his father."

Jack didn't, either, and Chloe clearly didn't think Ry had one. Which was maybe true. Maybe not. Either way, Chloe wasn't going to be too happy with this turn of events. She'd want to head over to the ranch right now, intervene.

"I also wanted to talk to Brink about what we found in the chest," Hart said. "Can you transfer me? She can call me back later if she's out on a call."

"Are you going to tell her about Mark?"

"No, Sheriff. I'm only even telling you as a courtesy. It's an active investigation into her father. The less she knows, the better off we'll be."

"She doesn't have a relationship with her father."

Hart was quiet for a few humming seconds. "Regardless. She'll be kept in the loop in what directly affects her."

It was a clear-enough warning. Jack wasn't supposed to tell her either. He didn't like how that settled in him like betrayal instead of just the nature of the job.

"It's almost shift change. She should be available. Stay on hold for a second." Jack got up and stepped out of his office and peeked into the main lobby, where his deputies met for shift change.

Chloe was at the front desk, smiling over something on

Suzanne's phone—probably the insane pictures Suzanne took of her cats dressed up like old Hollywood stars.

He hated to wipe that smile off her face, but when both Suzanne and Chloe looked over at him, he saw any enjoyment melt away. Because she knew it wasn't good news.

"Chloe, Detective Hart's on line one for you."

Chapter Ten

Jack shouldn't have called her Chloe in front of Suzanne. It was a dead giveaway. Maybe not to *everyone*, but Suzanne was not everyone. She had a keen eye, an even keener ear and a nose for things other people didn't want to share.

Jack had never once slipped up in front of anyone in all this time, and dread swept through her because she had a terrible feeling that Jack had used her first name because something really bad was just about to fall in her lap. Courtesy of Detective Hart.

Chloe wanted to ignore the call, run in the other direction, ask Jack to handle it. A million things that she wouldn't do, because whatever this was, it was all hers. Just like always.

She moved stiffly into one of the offices the deputies all shared, closed the door and gave herself a second to breathe before she lifted the phone receiver. Whatever it was, she could weather it. She'd gotten this far, hadn't she? "This is Brink."

"Hey. Detective Hart here. I just wanted to give you an update on what we found in that chest of yours."

Chloe swallowed, found a spot on the wall to stare at and made sure she sounded strong and firm. "Go ahead."

"Mostly, it was just the dolls. We're going to run some

tests on the smears—determine fake or real blood and go from there. Some weapons were hidden inside some of the dolls. We'll have to keep and run tests on those too. See if they were used in any of your father's known crimes."

"Great." She hoped she didn't sound *too* sarcastic.

"There was also an old scrapbook. Delaney-Carson and I both looked through it, and we don't see any reason for Bent County to keep it. It seems more family heirloom than anything else. Whenever you have a chance to stop by County, you can feel free to pick it up."

She didn't know whether she wanted to laugh or cry or just rage. All that—dolls and weapons—and her father hadn't even been fully lying. There *was* a family heirloom hidden in there.

She should tell Hart to throw it in the incinerator. "I'll be by tonight."

"Okay. It'll be up with Administration. You know the drill."

"Yeah, thanks." She returned the phone to its receiver. Then she just stood there, still staring at the same spot. She didn't have her cruiser here; that was at her cabin. Her personal car was at the Hudson Ranch. She did *not* want Jack driving her over there. She didn't know what kind of reaction she was going to have to this scrapbook, and she didn't want him witnessing it.

She didn't want anyone with her when she picked it up, when she inevitably went through it even knowing it was pointless. Whatever she wanted to find wasn't going to be in some old, dusty book that may or may not even actually be a Brink family scrapbook.

But regardless, she wanted to handle all that alone. Where

she didn't have to worry about how her reactions might affect how anyone viewed her.

She blew out a breath, closed her eyes and tried to find her lifelong inner toughness. That thing she'd been building up since she was a kid. She had known, always, that life was nothing more than a series of blows to dodge and absorb as needed. Any good, you carved out yourself with hard work and fierce grit.

Why was she having such a hard time with these blows?

A knock sounded at the door. Chloe didn't have to be psychic to know who it was. She twisted the knob and pulled it open.

Jack stepped in, closed the door behind him and studied her.

Here was the answer to the question. Where was her grit? Well, this man had somehow washed it away. By taking care. By *loving* her.

And what was it going to get her, this love? Ridicule? Pain? Guilt? And so much fear that it would all disappear, she didn't know how anyone lived with the weight of *love* you chose.

"Everything okay?" Jack asked carefully.

"Yeah." She realized that Jack had been the one to tell her Hart was on the phone, which meant he'd talked to Hart first. "I'm sure Hart filled you in on everything."

Jack shook his head. "No. Just that he wanted to talk to you about the contents of the chest."

She shrugged, still not ready to look at him. "Running tests. Found some weapons. Mostly called because they found some old family scrapbook, I guess. I can go pick it up sometime."

"I'll drive you."

She forced herself to look at him, to be *strong*. She had not gotten this far in life by being an emotional weakling or coward. She would *not* be cut down at the knees just because he loved her. "Look—"

But this was Jack. Did she think there'd be some way to get around that bullheaded need to control and protect?

I need you to let me. He'd said that to her like…like she had any say. Like he had wants or needs he couldn't expressly make happen in the Jack Hudson world of control and determination.

Like *she* had that kind of hold over him.

"Two-man until we have answers, Chloe," he said firmly. "And I don't just mean at work. If it's not me, you're going to have to ask Baker or Clinton to drive you over. Or we'll head back to the ranch, and you can take Ry with you later tonight. Or Mary."

She wanted to do just that—pick someone else—to prove to him she could. No. To prove to *herself* she could. To put some space between them when she had to do something she knew would be emotionally painful.

But he'd said he *loved* her.

She couldn't wrap her head around why that put her more on edge than when she'd believed the whole thing had been about sex and nothing else. When she had convinced herself he was *embarrassed* of her family connections. That had been easy because it had been anger, she supposed. Indignation. Hard feelings that kept her silly heart guarded.

Now it was just soft feelings and too much outside stuff poking at her to bear.

"I need space on this, Jack." She wasn't going to cry again. Once was enough, but she could feel emotion mounting. So she needed to set a boundary. Or five hundred.

"I can give you space," he said, nodding like he was agreeing with her even though she knew better. "You want to look through it alone? Your choice, Chloe. But *someone* is going to be with you at all times when you're off the ranch until we can rule out a threat to you."

I need you to let me. I need you to let me. It kept ringing in her head, over and over. Like it was something she could count on.

When she hadn't been able to count on anything aside from herself in her entire life.

"Let's just go get it over with," she managed to say, not crying but sounding raspy nonetheless.

He nodded again; then he reached out. Just a quick, friendly squeeze of the shoulder. "I need to grab a few things. I'll meet you at my truck."

She gave him a sharp nod, refusing to react to the hand on her shoulder, the softness in his gaze or anything else.

Just had to get through the day. She could fall apart— alone—tonight. Then maybe tomorrow she'd have answers for how to deal with everything life had thrown at her today.

She collected her own things, met Jack at his truck. They didn't speak. She didn't even look at him. She watched out the window as he drove away from Sunrise and toward…

She frowned and sat a little straighter. "This isn't the way to County," she said with a frown. She glanced over at him. He was gripping the wheel, scowling ahead.

"We're going to need to stop by the ranch first."

"Why?" she asked because he seemed so serious, so determined, and she didn't understand why.

His scowl deepened if that was possible. "Delaney-Carson is interviewing Ry again. I figured you'd want to be there."

"Why is she doing that?" Chloe leaned forward, nearly screeching out the demand.

"There are some concerns he has a relationship with your father." Jack let out a long breath. "Mark Brink was spotted in Denver the morning after the remains were found."

"He's in prison."

"He's on parole." Jack looked over at her then. "Hart made it very clear I wasn't supposed to share any of this with you, but I don't want you finding it out from anyone else."

Another rule broken, a line crossed for *her*, and Chloe couldn't handle that. Not right now. She had to handle the actual information. "So, he was in Denver? What does that…" But she was a cop. She understood how you built a case. If her father had been halfway between Texas and Wyoming the *morning* the remains had been found, they were thinking someone had warned him the remains were going to be found. *If* he was involved, *if* he'd been on his way to Wyoming.

Was it even an *if* anymore?

"Ry doesn't have any connection to our father." Her father had loved to play mind games with her, but he'd actually knocked Ry around some. Ry wouldn't…

But with drugs involved, there weren't a whole lot of things she could count on Ry *never* doing. Including this. He could have called their father before he'd called her. Her father could have told Ry to dig there, and Ry didn't mention it because he knew how she felt about Mark Brink.

There were a lot of *could*s. Too many.

When Jack pulled up to the ranch, she once again didn't want to face what awaited her, but she didn't have time to wish for different. The detective's car was parked out front. She was already inside, talking to Ry.

Chloe knew she should let her. Let Ry handle himself. But…

"Can you not come in with me? I don't want the detective to think we're like marching in as Sunrise Sheriff's Department, trying to take over—or worse, make a mess of her investigation. I just want to be there if Ry needs me. I'm not stopping anything." She said that last bit more for herself than Jack.

Jack nodded. "I'll go around back."

She swallowed what was beginning to feel like a perpetual lump in her throat. "Thanks." But before she could push out of the truck, Jack took her hand, held it in his and pressed their joined hands against his chest until she met his gaze.

Serious. So damn serious. "I know Ry's your responsibility, but he's not under your control, Chloe. Trust me, as a man who has spent the past seventeen years trying to control Anna's mouth, sometimes you just have to be there to catch them when they fall, not try to stop it from happening."

She wanted to be angry that he was trying to tell her what to do, but she saw it too clearly for what it was. Commiseration. She managed a nod, then to get her hand free. She got out of the truck, didn't look back at Jack. Just marched onto the porch and to the door, which was unlocked, so Chloe let herself in. It felt a little weird, but worry over Ry superseded any awkwardness she felt. She followed the sound of voices—Ry's agitated one—and found them in the living room.

Ry was pacing the room like a caged animal while Detective Delaney-Carson sat relaxed as could be on the couch. When Ry heard her enter, his chin snapped up.

"Chloe, why won't they leave me alone?" He pointed at the detective. "Isn't this harassment? I didn't do anything *wrong*."

"Okay," Chloe agreed, because there was no arguing with her brother when he was this agitated. She turned to the detective, tried to smile. "I thought you'd already questioned us, Detective."

She nodded. "Yes, but you know as well as I do when new information comes to light, a second, third or even fourth questioning might be necessary."

"What new information?"

The detective's expression bordered on disdainful now. "Deputy Brink, I'm not going to share—"

"She said Dad's out on parole and is acting like I know something about it or, like I'm hiding him or I don't know. But I didn't do anything wrong!"

Chloe wanted to melt into a puddle of embarrassment, but she kept her placid expression on her face as she faced the detective. "Are you charging my brother with anything?"

"No, Deputy. We're just asking when the last time he had contact with Mark Brink was, and answers have not been forthcoming."

Chloe tried to ignore her stomach sinking. If he wasn't answering... But she turned to her brother. No blame, no embarrassment, no frustration on her face. Just blank. "Ry," she said calmly, "it's a simple question. Even if you don't know the exact date, you have an idea. How long has it been?"

"You know Dad. He's not consistent. In one day, out the next. I don't remember talking to him since he went to prison, and I don't know why that's anyone's business, what it's got to do with those bones. I'm only twenty-four! You think I was a kid burying skeletons?"

"I don't think anything, Mr. Brink," the detective said, her voice on the chilly side. "And at the moment, you're hardly a murder suspect. What I am trying to do is gather information to solve a case. It would help if you could be cooperative instead of combative."

"You're accusing me of doing something wrong! You don't think I know how you people think? All your female-cop bull—"

"Rylan Jonas Brink," Chloe said sharply. Sharp enough that he was surprised into clamping his mouth shut. "That's enough. Now, are you saying you haven't had any contact with Dad since he went to prison?"

"I don't remember talking to him *once*," Ry grumbled.

Chloe turned to the detective, so tense it was a miracle her bones didn't simply shatter from the force of it all. "Do you have any more questions, Detective?" She expected to see fury or affront on the detective's face.

What Chloe saw was worse: pity.

"No. Not right now. Thank you, Deputy Brink. If I have any more questions, I'll let you know." She stood, but as she passed Chloe on the way out, she said something quietly enough so Ry couldn't hear. "If he changes his story, or if you find out something you think might help this investigation, I'd really appreciate it if you let me know. We all want the same thing here. Answers."

Chloe nodded jerkily. Because it was true. They all needed answers.

She stood in silence, watching her brother pace. She had no words. She had *nothing*. So she just watched him until he stopped pacing. Until he looked at her, all sheepish and sullen.

He was good at being angry, at blaming everyone around him, but he always broke in the face of her anger. Well, if he was sober.

"I'm sorry, Chloe," he said, crossing the room to her. "I didn't mean it. She just got me so riled up, poking at me with the same questions."

This was the problem with Ry. She believed he *was* sorry. In the moment. She just also believed he'd do it again and again because he wasn't sorry enough to change, to grow, to learn. He was determined to stay stuck in this everyone-else-is-to-blame place.

And she couldn't fix him.

She'd spent so many years trying to accept that. She wondered if she ever fully would be able to.

"How was working with Cash and Carlyle?" she asked, because she needed to make sure he hadn't ruined anything else today before she went back to the subject at hand.

He gave her a jerky shrug that reminded her of the little boy he'd been. She'd tried so hard to save him from everything, and she'd failed. "They have like a hundred of them."

"Of what?"

"Dogs." His mouth curved ever so slightly. "They didn't give us that speech in high school when they were telling us we had to think about our futures. Maybe if someone had told me, 'Hey, dog training is a thing people do,' I would have tried harder."

She didn't say anything to that, even though *she* had told him. *She* had tried to find any way of getting him to *care*, to put forth an effort. Vet school. Owning his own kennel or working on someone else's ranch. *Anything.*

But Ry had to blame someone else for where his life was. Always.

Which brought them right back to the subject at hand. "Ry, have you had *any* contact with Dad in the past year?"

"You heard what I told the detective."

"I did. And now I want you to look me in the eye and tell me that for an entire year, you haven't had a phone call, an email, a certified letter, nothing."

"I didn't do anything wrong," he said. Which was the third or fourth time she'd heard that in the last ten minutes. And didn't answer the question.

"Then what *did* you do?"

He stood there. Then slowly, his dark eyes filled with tears. "I'm sorry, Chloe. I really am."

Chapter Eleven

"He lied."

Jack looked up from the computer screen that had been giving him a hell of a headache. With Steve out and Chloe needing to ride two-man, adjusting the Sunrise SD work schedule was a hell of a puzzle he hadn't fully figured out yet. Even with him stepping in to cover daily shifts. So he didn't quite follow Chloe's dramatic statement. He only knew she was standing in the doorway, looking like a storm ready to break. "Who lied about what?"

"Ry lied to the detective."

Jack tried not to swear, tried to maintain a detached kind of calm that she no doubt needed, but he wasn't perfect. "Lied how?"

"All she wanted to know, allegedly, was if he'd had contact with Dad lately. He told her he hadn't talked to Dad since he went to prison, but he refused to hand over his phone, of course. And he kept saying he hadn't done anything wrong, and that's always when I know he has."

She looked up at Jack then. Tears swam in her eyes, but they didn't fall. "He's had contact with Dad over the past year. Text messages and emails." She raked her hands through her hair, loosening more strands from the once-tight braid she'd had at the beginning of the day.

"He said it didn't have anything to do with anything. Just father-son stuff. I can't believe he..." She was pacing the tiny office room. There was no room to pace, but she clearly couldn't sit still. Anger and frustration pumped off her, but underneath all that was the impossible pull of wanting to do the right thing for her family and needing to do the right thing for the law.

"I should have handled it better. I should have found a way to get him to admit it to the detective. He always lies when he's backed into a corner, and if I had—"

"You're not blaming yourself, are you? Because I know you know you're not to blame for Ry lying."

She took a breath and finally stopped pacing. She looked at him with heartbreak in her eyes. Then shook her head. "Bad habit."

"I know. So, let's work through this. He told the detective he hasn't had contact with your dad?"

She shook her head. "Oh, no, of course not. He said *I haven't talked to him* since he went to prison, so he's convinced it wasn't a *lie* because he only communicated in texts and emails. God, I'd like to strangle him."

"And he says these conversations were just generic. Did he let you see any of them?"

She shook her head. "He claims he left his phone at my cabin, and he'll show them to me later. I know he didn't, and I know he won't."

"So he is hiding something." Jack sighed. It just didn't add up. What would Ry be hiding? He'd been too young to really be involved in any kind of murder or coverup. Besides, if Mark Brink killed those people...

"He's protecting our father, for whatever godforsaken reason," Chloe said, clearly trying so hard to be strong. For what, he didn't know. Neither her father nor her brother really deserved that kind of dedication.

But even if they didn't, their behavior connecting to cold case murders didn't make sense either. "If Mark knew about the remains *before* Ry dug, how did Ry warn him before he dug? And if Ry knew your father committed those murders and is trying to cover for him, why would he dig there or anywhere? It doesn't make sense."

"I'm not sure what my father or brother does always adds up."

"Sure, but… We're missing something here. The timing doesn't work out for them to be purposefully covering up something Mark did that Ry knew about."

Chloe sucked in a breath. "We should let the detectives handle it. I'll tell them… I'll tell them…" She couldn't seem to get out the words. He hated why, but he understood it all the same.

"You don't want to tell Laurel what you know."

She looked up at him, her eyes still shiny, but clearly she had determined she wasn't going to cry over this. "Ry needs to be maneuvered. You can't just get answers out of him. And if there are answers to be had, I'm the best chance we have of getting them. If I involve the detectives, I just don't think it'll give us answers. Not without someone getting hurt."

She shoved her hands in her pockets, looked at some place on the wall just behind him, as if it'd give him the illusion she was making eye contact.

"I know it's wrong. I know I shouldn't still want to protect him. But he's not a murderer. Maybe Dad's wrapped him up in this but only because he knows how to manipulate him. Not because Ry did anything wrong. I mean, he did. He lied. I just…" She seemed to run out of words, or maybe they were lodged in her throat. Because she just stood there, looking miserable.

So he moved over to her. He pulled her close, rubbed his hand up and down her spine until *some* of that tension in her loosened. "Take a breath, Chloe. We'll work through it. One step at a time."

"I've got to stop laying this stuff at your feet. You're the real victim here. You and your family."

"Sounds like we're all victims."

She shook her head against his chest, but she didn't pull away from him. She let him hold her.

He figured if anything made sense about the two of them, it was this. They both felt they had to do it all, hold it all together, and because they did, the other was the only person they knew how to lean on.

"You shouldn't be comforting me. You've got your own awful stuff to deal with."

"Yeah, but mine is old, and while it's not *dealt* with, you went with me on that drive the other night. You hate heights, and you sat next to me and listened to me talk. Things I can't seem to admit to anyone else." He held her closer.

"But—"

He pulled her back so he could look into her gaze. He hadn't fully realized until all this had gone down how much she'd hidden from him in the past year. Old childhood hurts, insecurities. Trauma.

He'd had his own trauma, but he'd had a foundation to deal with it on. She'd had nothing but herself.

"All this bad stuff? It's not math. There's not a chart. You get to be upset. I get to be upset. And we'll comfort each other however we can. Love isn't a contest or a transaction, Chloe. It doesn't work that way."

Her chin wobbled, but she firmed it on an exhale. "I don't know how love works."

"Well, I guess you'll figure it out as we go."

She rolled her eyes, but not disdainfully. And she didn't pull fully away. But the misery was still in every line of her face.

"We need to get to the bottom of this, Jack. I don't want to go to Laurel, but you need answers. We all need answers."

"So we'll find them. Together."

"How?"

Maybe he'd been avoiding it, but he'd known, since this morning, since Chloe's safety had come into question, he couldn't play hands-off anymore. Not and live with himself.

"By making this a Hudson Siblings Solutions case."

CHLOE HAD HELPED the Hudson clan with cold cases before, but mostly in a very supplementary way: getting them information they couldn't get themselves, responding to active threats connected to their cold cases. But she'd never been involved in a full-fledged Hudson Sibling Solutions meeting.

It wasn't all that different from a family dinner. Everyone shoved together in the living room instead of the dining room. The low buzz of conversations, bickering and the most recent addition of a baby occasionally fussing while everyone arrived and got settled.

Carlyle was missing because she'd made up an excuse to use Ry to do some evening chores with her and Izzy out at the dog barns. Jack had offered to let Ry be part of the meeting, but Chloe had nixed that idea.

She loved her brother, wanted to protect him with all she was, even to the point of risking things she shouldn't risk, but she couldn't trust him with *anything*. Especially this. She might want to protect him from the repercussions of what he'd potentially done, but she wouldn't do it at the expense of finding the truth.

She didn't really think Ry had done anything wrong when it came to the skeletal remains, but she could see how any involvement with their father could mean he was mixed up in *something* wrong.

"This meeting better be about what I think it's about," Anna said, with baby Caroline situated on her lap.

The fringe conversations began to die out, and all eyes turned to Jack. Chloe had always known he'd taken on too much here with his family, felt a responsibility that was maybe bigger than necessary.

But she'd never so clearly seen it in action—everyone he loved turning their attention to him, looking to *him* for answers. Since he'd been eighteen years old. Her heart ached for the young man he'd been.

"The case regarding the skeletal remains—that, I'll point out, have not been positively IDed yet—has changed on us, gotten more complicated, and now it includes a potentially current threat."

"No one is threatening me," Chloe muttered, because for all that was mixed up and wrong, some mutilated snake on her porch with absolutely no information didn't lend itself to her being worried. The dolls in the chest were an old "joke" from her father. She didn't have any actual *fear* of a threat, but she was *letting* Jack take care of her.

Or trying to anyway.

"I think a mutilated snake on your porch is threat enough,

whether we know what it's threatening or not," Mary said primly.

"Maybe it doesn't connect. The snake. Mark Brink. The remains. But the timing feels like too much of a coincidence," Jack continued. "I still want us supporting Bent County detectives in all facets we can, but things have changed enough, I think we should launch our own investigation."

Chloe expected there to be *some* reaction from the Hudson siblings. A grim kind of excitement or relief that Jack was okaying what he'd previously forbidden.

But there was silence. Dahlia snuck a look at Grant. Palmer suddenly found the ceiling *very* interesting. Anna studied Caroline's socks as if they had the answers to the mysteries of the world on them.

Jack sighed. "So go on and get everything you've been gathering in secret and against my wishes. We're looking into it now. As a team."

"Thank God," Anna muttered. She looked over at Hawk, who got up and left the room. One person from every couple did the same, slowly returning with arms full of things. One by one, they dropped files, notebooks and printouts onto the table in the center of the room in front of Jack. Chloe's eyes widened as it became a tower of papers that nearly toppled over. She snuck a glance at Jack.

He didn't look the least bit surprised. Resigned, a little disapproving, but maybe even just a *hint* of pride.

Chloe realized then that he'd known they were doing it. Behind his back. Even though he didn't want them to. And he wasn't angry about it.

Something about him knowing and just…letting them, even when he didn't want them to. It settled in her like warmth. Everyone painted him as so rigid, and he *could* be on the outside, but on the inside...

He was someone else entirely. And she loved him so much, it turned into *anxiety* inside her. Because love could so easily be taken away. Especially with a last name like hers.

"I haven't put it in my notes yet, but I *may* have eavesdropped when Detective Delaney-Carson interviewed Ry again," Anna said. She looked over at Chloe. "He's lying."

Chloe nodded. "I know." She swallowed. She didn't want to share with *all* of them what she'd found out, because she wasn't sure they would agree with Jack that they should *all* work together.

And she wanted to protect Ry, but in the audience of everyone whose parents might be buried on her family ranch, she felt the need to be honest. Even at Ry's expense.

"He admitted to me he's had written contact with our father. I haven't figured out what they talked about yet, but I'm going to." She took a deep breath. "And I'll make sure to share it with you as it pertains to the skeletal remains, but I also understand this is complicated. Well, that *I* make it complicated. Threats or no, we're looking at my father and a ranch my name is on. I understand if there's a thread of mistrust here, and I don't have to stay."

Jack gave her a sharp look, but it was nothing on Mary's.

"Chloe Brink, I have known you since we were in kindergarten. And not once, in all that time, all those different phases of our lives, have I ever thought you were *anything* like your father or your brother."

Before Chloe could respond to that, Palmer spoke. Because Chloe knew that for all Jack and Mary were on her side, it wasn't unanimous. Palmer had made it quite clear he had his doubts about her.

"It doesn't matter if she's like them if she's more worried about protecting them than getting to the truth," Palmer said. He didn't budge when both Jack and Mary glared at him. He sat where he was, looking right at Chloe. "I don't have anything against you as a person, Chloe, but your involvement is complicated."

"I agree. That's why I'm saying I don't have to be here."

Mary and Jack immediately began to argue with her. Anna looked to be on the fence, while Cash and Grant said nothing. The significant others didn't add anything at first, but eventually, when the arguing was clearly going nowhere, Louisa cut through all the chatter.

Chloe looked over at her. She was gripping Palmer's hand. Clearly they'd had a few discussions about this.

"The real question is this," Louisa said once everyone looked over at her. "If you found something implicating your brother, would you turn him in?"

Chloe turned her gaze from Louisa to Palmer. He looked so much like Jack, was *nothing* like his older brother. Except in this. That stoic, stern expression.

She could lie. She could be a good liar when she wanted to be. Hell, she lied to herself on a daily basis. But she shrugged. "I really don't know. It would depend on the situation."

Palmer leaned back in his seat, flung his arm over Louisa's shoulders. "Then my vote is that you stay."

Chloe had already started standing up to leave before the words penetrated. "Wait, what?"

"You were honest. That's all that really matters. We can't have secrets in an investigation, but siblings... I wouldn't believe you if you'd said yes. But an *I don't know*? That, I get. God knows I thought I'd have to cover up for Anna committing a crime at some point in our lives."

"You mean, you haven't?" Hawk murmured.

Anna put her hands over Caroline's ears. "Not in front of the *baby*," she said with mock seriousness. "She's going to grow up thinking her mother is a saint."

This elicited a laugh from just about everyone in the room. A laugh. While they were sitting around talking about their parents' disappearance and potential murder. Her family's involvement in such a tragedy.

But, Chloe realized, here in a room where all the Hudsons were gathered—but not just Hudsons. Significant others and offspring too. Seventeen years of unknowns while life marched on had meant probably figuring out... you couldn't live your life constantly mired in that old tragedy.

So maybe she should stop living mired in the reputation other people had given her last name.

Chapter Twelve

They went over it all. The old information the police had gathered when their parents had disappeared, what his siblings had gathered in the past few days. Nothing new, nothing groundbreaking, but it was good to talk it through.

Jack was trying to convince himself it was good. He knew it wasn't true, but he *felt* like the only one struggling with the weight of what they were discussing. Not just anyone's skeletal remains—his parents.

Not positively IDed yet, he reminded himself. Or tried to.

Though they'd all done some of their own investigating over the years, there wasn't anything really new so far. Anna and Palmer had both been looking into any connection Mark Brink might have had to their parents. Mary had been looking through old ranch records to see if something jumped out connecting anything Hudson to the Brink Ranch. Cash had been working with Zeke and Zeke's connections to see if he could get more information on the crime scene as it was right now.

"So, we did all this and we're still in the same exact spot?" Anna groused.

"It's not the same exact spot," Mary said, clearly trying to sound optimistic. "Just like any cold case. We don't know which corner might lead us to a new thread. So we keep going. I still have old ranch records to look through, and we don't know what the forensic anthropologist might have to say. It's a step."

"It's a foolish step," Anna muttered.

"I think that's a sign someone is tired," Hawk said, earning a scowl from his wife. "Mary's right. We've got next steps. Let's call this a night. Caroline's conked out anyway," he said, gesturing to the sleeping baby in Anna's arms.

She sighed and got to her feet, and everyone else began to disperse, couple by couple.

Chloe stood. "I better go check on Ry. Make sure Carlyle hasn't scarred him for life." She tried to smile. It faltered.

"Did you want to go get that scrapbook?" Jack asked.

She waved it off, already heading out of the room. "Tomorrow morning is soon enough," she muttered. Then she disappeared. Jack wanted to follow her, but Mary started tidying up, so both he and Grant stepped in to stop her.

"Go to bed, Mary. We can clean up."

She frowned at them both, hands on her hips, but Walker urged her out of the room so that it was just Jack and Grant collecting debris. Jack figured they'd work in quiet. Grant usually did.

"So, how long has your thing with Chloe been going on?"

If it had been anyone else standing there asking him that question, Jack would have had a quick answer. An easy lie. He expected things like that from just about everyone.

But never Grant.

Grant, who most people would never guess was *married* to his wife, because he and Dahlia were so private they almost never engaged in even *hand holding* in front of people. Grant, who'd taken *eons* to propose to Dahlia, if compared to Mary, Anna and Palmer's quick jumps into commitment. Who'd had a wedding so small, it had only been immediate family because they hadn't wanted an audience.

"What?" was all Jack managed.

But Grant didn't relent. *Grant*. The man who'd returned from war and kept every last effect of that to himself. No matter how obvious they'd been.

"I can repeat myself if you really need me to, but I think you know what I asked." He calmly stacked papers together.

"Who are you, and what have you done with my brother?" Grant, who was closest in age to Jack, who'd been his kind of right-hand man in keeping everything together that first year. Because he'd been the only one old enough to also drive. He'd helped with school runs and sports practices. If it hadn't been for Grant, who'd been *sixteen*, Jack would have fumbled the whole thing.

Grant's mouth curved ever so slightly. "It's a simple question, Jack. I know a lot about all the things a person tells themself that doesn't serve them. We'd hate to think you have to keep yourself some isolated paragon for the rest of us."

Jack wanted to be touched that Grant was concerned about him, but… "'We'?"

Grant's expression went *almost* sheepish. "It's been a topic of conversation."

"With *who*?"

"Well, I think it started with Carlyle, then it kind of spread from there. Not everyone believed it at first. Dahlia was an early believer though, and it's hard to argue with her. She observes things. Cash and Walker weren't so easily swayed, but recently…" Grant shrugged. "I think the lone holdout on that score is Palmer. He's convinced you'd *never* cross a line at work."

Jack wasn't sure what was worse: all the people who thought it was true or the fact Palmer was wrong about him.

"So you guys have been sitting around debating whether or not I have a relationship with Chloe?"

"You do know your family, right? And Carlyle? She brings it up every chance she gets. She's determined to be right. She is, isn't she?"

"Are you going to take my answer back to the collective?" Jack returned, a little bitterly even to his own ears.

"I don't have to. I can keep a secret." He shrugged as if it was that simple. And Jack wasn't sure if it was just who Grant was or because they were the closest that Grant was probably the only one he'd believe that from.

"I just didn't want you laboring under the assumption you weren't allowed to have a life too. Taking care of everyone has been your life for so long. I'm sure it's hard to realize we're all grown up and let that go. But we are. And we're all here. We're all good."

"It isn't that," Jack managed, though it wasn't so fully off the mark, he realized. "Maybe it was a little in the beginning, but… Working together complicates things. For Chloe."

"Life is complicated. You can't protect everyone, Jack."

He was a little tired of that getting thrown in his face at every turn, but… "I can try."

Grant shook his head, but he didn't argue. "Look, asking you about Chloe isn't the only thing I wanted to talk to you alone about."

"You want to probe deeper into my sex life for the past decade?"

Grant pulled a face, as Jack had hoped. He hadn't learned *nothing* from being Anna's older brother.

"No," Grant said stoutly. "We're not really telling everyone yet, but I figured you should be the first to know."

"Know what?" Maybe he should have seen it coming. Grant wasn't the first, but Jack was really taken off guard by Grant's next words.

"Dahlia's pregnant."

It shouldn't be a shock. Kids were going to follow marriage more often than not, but maybe Jack thought Grant would feel a little like he did. Like he'd already raised a family.

But Grant's mouth was curved, as wide as Grant ever smiled. Happy. Grant Hudson, war hero, married and starting a family.

Jack really didn't know how to absorb it, but what he tried to do in these kinds of moments was think back to their father. What would he have done?

But in this case, Jack didn't know. Because his father had never had the chance to parent *adults*. The idea of being a grandfather had probably never been one he'd entertained for too long, too busy getting his six kids grown first.

So Jack just had to rely on himself. He reached out, gave Grant's shoulder a squeeze. "You'll make a hell of a father, Grant. You've had some hands-on practice."

He shrugged. "Had some good role models to follow too." He patted Jack on the shoulder, like *he* was one of them. "You don't have to pretend with Chloe around us. No one's going to cause a problem here. Seems to me you guys should have *somewhere* you don't have to pretend."

"I'll, uh, talk to Chloe about it. Not sure how comfortable she'd be."

"Sure. I'll keep my mouth shut."

"Even to Dahlia?"

"Well, maybe not that shut. But she won't tell anyone. You have my word."

And Grant's word was good as gold. Always had been.

Jack didn't think he'd had much to do with that, but maybe…maybe some. A tiny, little bit. And it made him feel pretty damn good that he had.

CHLOE FOUND RY laughing with the dogs. Carlyle was watching them with an eagle eye, but from a distance. Giving Ry the illusion of being in charge.

It made her heart twist that it looked like he was handling it just fine. Why hadn't *she* been able to keep him out of trouble?

Well, didn't do to think about now. She walked over to Carlyle first. "Hey. How's it going?"

"As long as the animals are around? He's fine. Not irritating at all. Might have wanted to pound him on the walk over while he was whining about his tough lot in life— please, buddy, I win. Still, I think we'll be able to keep him busy and out of trouble without a pounding."

"I can't tell you how much I—"

Carlyle held up a hand. "Don't thank me. It's rude."

"How is thanking you rude?"

"Because it is," Carlyle replied. Then she gave Chloe a kind of sideways look. "So, is this whole protect-you-on-the-Hudson-Ranch thing Jack Hudson's version of trying to get in your pants?"

Chloe choked on a sharp inhale. "What? No!"

"Is that because he's already in your pants?"

"Carlyle!"

"So *that's* a yes." Carlyle looked back at Ry, who was getting the dogs into the barn one by one. "I *knew* it."

Chloe knew if there was anyone she'd slipped up around when it came to *maybe* hinting she had a thing for Jack, it was Carlyle and only Carlyle. But... "You did not."

"I totally knew it. I just couldn't figure out why all the secrecy about it."

Chloe could hedge, lie, make up a story, but she was tired and emotionally wrung out, and hell, Carlyle was her friend. "He didn't want to tell anyone because he didn't want to see me get needled at work over it."

"Aw. That's actually sweet. You know, at first I thought he was kind of a cold fish, but he's grown on me. He's just like all uptight goody-two-shoes because he's always trying to make everything right. It's annoying as all get out, but it's kind of sweet when it doesn't tick me off."

Chloe shrugged jerkily. Sure, it was. That's why it was so damn unnerving. "Well, anyway. We still work together, so—"

"Weren't you applying for that K-9 job at Bent County?"

Chloe pulled a face. She hadn't told anyone about that... except Carlyle after a few too many at the Lariat one night.

"I'm not going to apply for some job just to... Whatever."

"No, you were going to apply for it because you love dogs and were getting tired of the same old same old in Sunrise."

Chloe hadn't hit Submit on the application because as much as she wanted to try her hand at the K-9 unit in Bent County, she hadn't wanted Jack or anyone else to read into her switching jobs. One way or another. Because she'd needed to prove to herself she was strong enough not to go switch jobs in the hopes she'd have a future with *some guy*.

"No one will think that I'm moving jobs because I want a different job when my relationship with Jack gets out. They'll think I'm weak and lovesick," she muttered.

Carlyle looked at her like she'd grown a second head. "What does it matter what anyone else thinks? You *do* want a different job. And you're about as weak as a boulder."

Yes, but that's not what this was about. It was… It was… something. Carlyle just didn't… "You don't understand what it's like to grow up in a small town."

"No, but I do understand what it's like to be a grown up, Chloe. What other people think only matters if you let it."

It frustrated her because she didn't know how to argue with it. And with everything else going on, she wasn't handling that as well as she should. "Well, thanks for that after-school special, Car, but I've still got to drive over to Bent County and pick some of my confiscated belongings up." She didn't want to wait until morning now. She wanted to get out and away. From everyone. "I'll deliver Ry back to his room."

Carlyle shook her head. "Leave him. Cash is going to have him pick out a dog to keep him company inside once he's got Izzy to bed. We'll handle it."

"You don't need—"

"Chloe."

"What?"

"Scram."

"Carlyle, he's my brother and my—"

"Burden? Cool. We'll handle it for a while. And if you keep arguing with me, I'm literally going to fight you."

Chloe glared at Carlyle, but also wouldn't put it past the woman. And she was feeling so…so…twisted up, she couldn't find any words to get through to Carlyle. So she left. Left her brother as someone else's responsibility.

The Hudsons and their extended little network wanted to take over her life? Fine. They wanted to take care of her lying, unpredictable brother? Great. They wanted to watch her every move because of some nonsense threat that *Jack* perceived there to be? Let them.

She didn't know why it was getting harder and harder to breathe. Like there was a pressure in her chest, so heavy that she couldn't even fill up her lungs. It was all too much like impending doom.

Because they couldn't handle *everything* for her. *Something* was going to crash and burn, and then it'd be all up to her again—and then what?

She was going to leave. Right now. Just get in her car and go. Get the scrapbook and then head home. *Her* home. She didn't want to be protected. She didn't want to be helped. She wanted…

She started to change her route. Walk for the front, where her car was parked, instead of the side door that would lead her back into the house. To Jack.

Jack. Who *loved* her for some reason. Who'd asked her to let him take care of her. Because *he* needed that.

She swore and stopped walking, right there in the middle of the yard, starlight sparkling all around her. She couldn't be that woman who just took off. Oh, she wanted to be. *God*, she wanted to be. But it would hurt him if she went off by herself, and even if she didn't think she was in any danger, all it would take is for one little thing to go off course for her to feel like she'd been wrong.

She turned back toward the house, and then there he

was. Stepping out of the side door, the porch light shining a little halo around his head.

She loved him so much, it made her want to run away. Because what he didn't understand was that for all the ways she presented herself, for all the ways she thought therapy had helped her deal with her childhood trauma, deep down she saw—clearly, for the first time—how scared she was that it all just made her as unlovable as she'd always been treated.

But she *had* gone to therapy. She *had* faced a garbage fest of a childhood and worked on healing from those wounds. Maybe she wasn't all the way there, but it was about progress. Not perfection.

She walked over to him, not sure what to say or even who to be. It was like Ry unearthing all those bodies hadn't just caused a major issue. It was like it had turned her life inside out and nothing made sense anymore.

Least of all the man on the porch. No, least of all *herself*.

"Were you going somewhere?" he asked. Not with accusation. Not with anger. He likely felt a little bit of those things, but he didn't use them on her. That wasn't him.

So she told him the truth. No lie would form. "Thought about taking off."

"What changed your mind?"

She took the stairs, got close enough to him that she could see the way he watched her. Maybe there was a little flare of irritation lurking in his dark eyes, but mostly the only thing on his face was worry.

She leaned forward against him, wrapped her arms around him. "You."

He ran a hand over her hair. A sweet, protective gesture as he pressed a kiss to her temple. "Good."

That simple response almost made her laugh. But this whole *day* also revealed a truth that she was going to have to accept.

Everything was going to feel off-kilter and wrong until they got to the bottom of this mystery that connected to both their pasts. "Let's go get that scrapbook. I think I need to not have it hanging over my head."

He nodded. "Keys in my pocket. Let's head out."

He drove out to Bent County. They didn't really talk, just listened to the low strains of the old-fashioned country music he preferred. It suited the mood. Sad, mournful, a little weird.

When he parked and turned off the engine, he got out with her. It wasn't a surprise, exactly, but she had to fight the knee-jerk desire to tell him to stay in his truck.

They walked in together, smiled at the administrative assistant behind the desk. Sunrise worked with Bent County enough for Chloe to know everyone here by name.

"Hey, Linda. I'm here to pick up the relinquished property Hart left for me."

Linda tilted her head. "I'm sorry, Deputy Brink. Hart hasn't told me about any relinquished property. I don't think he's here, but Laurel is. Let me call her down." She lifted a phone to her ear.

Something didn't set right with that. Chloe looked up at Jack. He was frowning. But they didn't say anything, just waited for Detective Delaney-Carson.

A few minutes later, she strode into the lobby area. She stopped short and looked at both of them like she was surprised to see them there. "What are you two doing here?"

"Picking up the scrapbook Hart called me about this afternoon."

The detective's eyebrows drew together. "He told me he was going to drive it out to you before he went home."

Chloe exchanged a look with Jack. "That's not what he told us. He said I could pick it up whenever."

She nodded. "That was our original plan, but when you didn't show up, he was going to drop it by the ranch."

"Maybe take a pass at questioning Ry if he got the opportunity?" Jack offered, *sounding* casual.

Laurel studied Jack as if deciding what to say. Then she gave a little nod. "Yeah. Did he?"

"He never came by. Scrapbook or no."

Laurel's expression went from a puzzled kind of professionalism to flat-out worry. "I'll call him."

She took the phone Linda handed her, dialed the number and then waited. Her expression went from worry to cool, cop professionalism. But Chloe knew that meant something was *wrong*.

"He's not answering."

Chapter Thirteen

"Linda, can you get Hart's location? I'll take my cruiser and see if he stopped at home." The detective spoke calmly, smiled at the woman behind the desk. She gave no outward signs of distress or worry, but Jack could read it on her all the same.

Because this was out of the norm, and he knew *he* didn't like it, and he wasn't even Hart's partner.

"What can we do?" he asked her.

"Go home, Sheriff," Laurel said sharply, but when she turned to walk back into the station, Jack followed and so did Chloe.

"You've got two Sunrise deputies right here. Let us help."

"Sheriff, you know as well as I do you're both too involved in whatever this is to help in a professional capacity."

"I actually don't know that," Jack replied.

"Besides, I'm sure there's a reasonable explanation for all this," she continued, clearly ignoring him. But she didn't stop them from following her out the back exit of the station into the parking lot, which had personal cars and cruisers littered throughout.

Laurel strode toward some point only she knew, but then she came to an abrupt halt. In the dark, under the parking lot lights, one cruiser sat with its driver's-side door wide open. For a strange moment, they all stood there in stunned silence, looking at it.

"One of you go inside and tell Linda to get security footage of the parking lot up," Laurel said, her voice dead calm though she'd gone a little pale.

Chloe immediately turned and jogged back inside. Jack stayed with Laurel.

"How long would that have been like that without anyone noticing? Not long, right?"

Laurel shook her head as she approached the car. "Hard to say. Hart told me he was leaving about an hour ago. There hasn't been a shift change, so it's possible no one's been out here, but it's also possible he didn't leave right after he told me."

Jack peered into the open door of the car. There didn't seem to be signs of a struggle, but it was shadowy and dark in the car. Jack pulled out his phone and switched on the flashlight mode at the same time Laurel did.

Nothing appeared amiss, really, aside from the wide-open door. "Maybe he just forgot something?" It seemed like a leap—but then again, so did immediately jumping to conclusions about an open car door.

"No reason to leave the door open and kill the battery. Unless it was some kind of emergency." Laurel did a slow turn, eyeing the entire parking lot illuminated only by a few light towers. "It was still light out when he told me he was leaving. He's not… Whatever this is, it's not like him. *Something* happened."

Jack did his own looking around the parking lot. Bent County was hardly a bustling metropolis. Even though there was a police station right there, it wouldn't be impossible for something to happen out here and no one would see. Even if it was light out.

"He didn't get taken out of the police station's parking lot in broad daylight without someone seeing," Laurel said disgustedly, clearly more to herself than to Jack. "Without some kind of struggle. I don't know what this is, but it's not that."

Jack could hear what she was really doing: trying to talk herself out of thinking the worst. All while the worst was sitting right there in front of them.

"The footage is going to give us the answers we need. Let's go watch it."

"I don't like this," she muttered. "I told him we should have kept that scrapbook. It's all part of the Brink case. Not that I should be telling you this. Why are you even here?"

"Chloe might be a deputy at my department, but—"

"Come on, Sheriff. She's a lot more than your deputy. Anyone with eyes can see that."

Before Jack could react to *that*, Laurel was striding inside. Chloe met them halfway down the hall. "Linda says they're getting the footage up on the second floor."

Laurel looked at Chloe, then at Jack, then sighed. "All right, follow me." She took them up a set of stairs and then into a larger room clearly used for meetings. A man Jack recognized, though couldn't quite come up with a name, sat at a laptop.

He eyed Chloe and Jack, then Laurel. "Want me to put it up on the screen?"

Laurel nodded. In a few seconds, security footage of the police station parking lot showed up on the screen.

"What time you want?" he asked Laurel.

"Let's start at six. That's a little before when he told me he was leaving."

The footage sped up, people coming and going in quick time. When the man hit Play, the parking lot was empty aside from cars. Then Hart appeared. He had a box tucked under his arm.

"That's the scrapbook," Laurel explained, pointing to the box.

Hart opened his cruiser door, leaned in and put the box down, presumably on the passenger seat, though that wasn't fully visible from the camera angle. Then, before he slid into the driver's seat, he stopped, straightened and looked off into the distance with a puzzled frown.

Everyone held their breath as he turned and immediately began to jog off to the right—and quickly off-screen.

"We need footage of that side of the building," Laurel instructed the man at the computer.

"That side's a dead zone, Detective. We've only got cameras at entrances and exits—there aren't any in that corner."

Laurel swore.

"Does he see something, or does someone call out to him?" Chloe said, pointing to the screen. "Because he was getting in, but something stopped him. So someone had to have seen him. Something had to have gotten his attention."

"It's got to be a noise, right?" Jack returned. "He's getting ready to get *in* the car. Head down, then he looks over."

"But he leaves the scrapbook," Laurel added. "Keep rolling the footage," she told the man. "Because that scrapbook isn't there anymore."

Which meant sometime between when Hart went out of the parking lot and Jack and Laurel went out to the car, someone took it.

They watched. No one suggested they fast-forward the footage. They'd all investigated too many cases to let impatience get in the way of good police work. Seconds seemed to drag by, and tension settled into the air like a lead weight, wrapping around each of them as *nothing* happened on the screen. Minutes of just the trees blowing in the breeze and the sun slowly setting.

And then, *finally*, something showed up on the screen. A small figure, shrouded in a dark hoodie, moved quietly and stealthily up to the car, scooped up the scrapbook, and walked off the opposite side of the screen.

Laurel swore again. "I knew we should have kept it." She glared at Chloe. "What's in it?"

"How the hell should I know? I didn't even know it was in that chest."

"It's been in her garage, undisturbed for years. Anyone who wanted it could have gotten it easily. For years."

"Not if the person who wanted it was in prison," Laurel returned.

"If my father wanted it, he knew where it was and how to get to it. He could have sent Ry, and I wouldn't have thought twice about my brother hanging around my place. Detective, you can look into my father for anything you want, but it doesn't make sense to bark up that tree right now."

Laurel was still scowling, but she didn't argue with Chloe. "Here's what's going to happen: you're going to go back home and let me do my job."

"Who else is briefed on the case besides you?" Jack demanded.

Laurel's expression was stern. "I'll catch them up."

"We're going to look for him, Detective. With or without your permission or cooperation."

"I could have you arrested for tampering with an ongoing investigation."

Jack didn't take offense to the threat. He understood all too well what it was like to have no answers and someone you cared about in the middle of confusing danger. But he didn't bend either. "Or you could just let us help."

THEY WERE GIVEN the grunt job. They had trailed after Laurel as she'd gone from department to department, barking out orders. Then, when she'd finally stopped and turned to them, she'd told them to go search Hart's house.

Which was the grunt job because clearly Hart wasn't likely to have been there since before his shift today. Still, it was a necessary job, and Chloe and Jack drove from the police station over to Bent proper.

She couldn't blame the detective for keeping her out of most of it. Someone was going to call that parole officer in Texas and see where her father was, and if he wasn't verifiably in Texas tonight, he would be a top suspect.

But it didn't add up. Not to Chloe. Her father was shady as all get out, but he could have gotten that scrapbook whenever he wanted.

"There's something off here, Jack," she said, scanning the quiet street where Thomas Hart lived. She didn't know much about Thomas Hart's personal life, but according to Laurel, he lived alone in the little house they pulled up to.

A neat yard with no frills. A well-kept house with a porch light on in the dark.

Jack stopped the truck, and they both got out and studied the house from the front in what little light the porch and streetlamp offered.

"There's a lot of things off here, I think," Jack replied. "You don't have your gun on you. I want you to—"

"Follow behind. I know," she muttered, following him up to the porch. They'd knock on the front, then check around back. But Chloe didn't think they'd find anything here.

"The only person who knew about that scrapbook, far as I know, is my father. Nothing happened to it when it was only my father knowing. So what happened? Who got wind of it being with the cops?"

"Maybe that was the problem," Jack replied, rapping on the door. "Your father didn't want it with the police."

"I *am* the police."

Jack just shook his head as they waited. Chloe peered in the sidelight while Jack studied the front window, looking for a glimpse of anything. No one answered the door, no flicker of light or movement of curtains. Just stillness and silence.

Jack jerked his head, and Chloe nodded. They'd move around the east side of the house now. The street was quiet, the night heavy. As they moved around the side of the house, Chloe's nerves began to hum. In the front, the quiet had seemed like a comfortable small-town evening, but things were darker around back. Chloe kept even closer to Jack.

There were no lights on back here, so the postage stamp backyards all ran together like one big shadow. Some houses had lights on inside, shining in little cracks around curtains, but not many.

Jack pulled out a flashlight he must have grabbed from his truck. The beam shone across the grass, to a nice patio equipped with a ridiculously complicated-looking grill and then to a sliding glass door on the back of the house. Another curtain pulled tight. No lights here either.

"He's not here," Chloe said in a whisper. Not because they really needed to whisper, but because the night seemed to call for it.

"No."

But before they could discuss it further, something beeped, and it was so incongruous to the quiet night around them that Chloe nearly screamed.

Funny how she could almost always put her cop hat on, put the fear of danger to the side, but something about this case involving her father in *any* way made her feel more like the little girl who'd been terrified of him and less like the woman she'd built herself into.

He wasn't even *here*.

Jack pulled his phone out of his pocket. Someone was *calling* him, because little pinging noises were hardly her father jumping out of the shadows to be her own personal bogeyman.

Jack answered, and Chloe could hear the faint hum of a female voice on the other line but not the actual words. And still, something about the way Jack held himself told her it was bad news.

"Thanks, Mary. Keep me updated."

He turned to her in the dark. She couldn't make out the expression on his face, but he touched her shoulder.

Bad, *bad* news.

"Ry's missing."

She didn't know what she'd been expecting. But not that. She *should* have expected it, but somehow it took the wind right out of her. "But…" No *but*s. That's what Ry did.

She always screwed it all up, no matter how hard she tried.

"I'm sorry, Chloe."

She shook her head, not that he could see it in the dark. Maybe it took her off guard in *this* moment, but she'd also been ready for this in the long run. "I can track his phone. Maybe." She pulled her own phone out of her pocket, ignoring the way her hand shook. "I wasn't about to leave it up to chance. It's something I used to do when he was in high school, and I was trying to keep him in school. I haven't done it for years, so I was hoping he wouldn't notice and turn it off." She clicked the screen on her phone, brought up the location tracker and hoped.

The map moved around, zooming into a spot. Chloe would have felt immense relief, but he was in the middle of a campground by the mountains.

Not just any campground.

"That's where my parents were camping the night they disappeared," Jack said, his voice devoid of any and all emotion.

Chloe felt like her chest was caving in, but she didn't let it show. Couldn't. "If you don't want to go there, we can—"

"I'm going," Jack said sharply. But his voice softened on the next words. "This might connect, Chloe. Ry. The scrapbook. Hart missing. We can let someone else lead this. One of our guys. One of theirs. I can take you back to the ranch, but—"

Chloe shook her head. She had always protected her brother, would always want to, but now, in this moment, she realized if he was really involved in this… She wouldn't be able to stomach getting him out of it.

She took Jack's arm and pulled him back toward the truck. "Let's go."

Chapter Fourteen

Jack drove out to the campground he hadn't been at in a very long time. For the first few years after his parents' disappearance, he'd scoured every inch. Over and over again, with any free moment he had—which weren't many, when he'd essentially been raising five kids. But he'd found time.

He'd always found time. No doubt his siblings had as well. Always so sure there had to be an answer here. But that answer had never been found. Even now, knowing those skeletal remains were likely his parents, it didn't feel like answers were really within reach. Just farther and farther away.

It didn't bother him as much as he'd thought it would. He hadn't been fully cognizant of how the past few years had changed him. Even if now he could pinpoint it back to a moment.

Grant had finally left the military and come home for good a few years ago. That had been such a relief, not just for him but for the entire family. Tragedy hadn't struck again. Someone else in their family hadn't been here one day and gone the next.

Jack hadn't done more than glance at his parents' case since. He hadn't even driven down the road that led to the forest preserve. Maybe not consciously, but he'd avoided poking at that old wound in the same ways he'd been doing up to that point.

He didn't know if anyone else had felt that way. He wasn't even sure he'd fully realized it until this moment, driving into the forest preserve, realizing how much of his parents' case he'd put away.

Because somehow all the Hudson kids had made it into adulthood, not unscathed but alive. Building lives and families all their own. Digging into old tragedies felt like begging for trouble.

Yes, someone deserved to pay for what had happened to his parents. He still hoped someone *would*.

But what would be the cost?

It didn't matter. Answers or no. Trouble was here, in the shape of skeletal remains, missing detectives, the woman he loved and her runaway brother. So he had to see it through.

They didn't call Bent County. Jack knew they should. They were possibly going into something dangerous, and doing so without backup and without every local law enforcement agency having the information was risky. A risk neither of them should be taking. A risk he'd never take.

If it wasn't for her.

He drove, and neither of them suggested calling it in. Neither of them suggested anything. Chloe was as silent as he was. She was no doubt dealing with her own demons. Because Ry taking off *around* the same time Hart disappeared into presumably thin air felt ominous—connected, even if he couldn't see how. And there was no doubt in Jack's mind that Ry's disappearance was why neither of them were calling it in.

Bringing in other people would make it harder to protect Ry, no matter how little he deserved protecting.

When Chloe finally spoke, it was to give him directions to follow different twists and turns in the dirt road to find Ry's location somewhere within the preserve. Not too deep in it, or they'd be losing reception, and they wouldn't be able to track Ry's location if he didn't have service either, so that was good.

"Maybe we should approach on foot," Jack suggested when Chloe said they were getting close. "Gives us the element of surprise to really figure out what's going on here before Ry or whoever knows someone is coming."

"Yeah," Chloe agreed. Jack pulled off the road on the dirt shoulder. He turned off the car. "Grab the flashlight. I've got the only gun, so I want—"

"Me to stay behind. I know, Jack."

She didn't snap it. She sounded so defeated, it was like a little stab to his heart. That so many people in her life had failed her and lead her to all *this* mess, and she'd held up so well to all of it, but when did it get to be too much?

Jack knew there was nothing he could say about Ry, about her father, about *her* that could make this better. He hated that he couldn't do something to make this okay.

But there was no way to fix it, so they got out of the truck. Quietly, she came around to his side. She had her phone on, and the screen illuminated her face. She didn't look *affected* by what was going on, but her usual cop face had an air of exhaustion to it.

She switched on the flashlight from his truck and moved the beam around in front of them. "I think if we follow this road, then take the first right we come across, it'll lead us to him."

She didn't mention the possibility it wasn't Ry himself. That they could stumble upon just his phone and nothing else. So Jack didn't either. Why verbalize what they both knew?

"Got it," he replied instead. He followed the beam of light she held, making sure she stayed behind him enough that he felt reasonably sure he could stop anything unexpected from hurting her.

They moved in quiet precision. Jack was sure they were both trying to keep their minds blank, pretend like it was any Sunrise Sheriff Department case. Nothing that involved his parents or her brother.

When the flashlight beam illuminated a turn in the dirt road, Jack took it. They quickly found it wasn't actually a road, just a path to a parking area. Chloe came up next to him, sweeping her light around the dirt in front of them. Stopping when it landed on the lone car parked in the lot.

A car Jack recognized. Chloe's car.

Jack lifted his gun, looking around what little of the parking lot he could see in just the flashlight beam. It seemed to be deserted aside from the car. He glanced over at Chloe, who would be hurt by this. No matter what it was. Her brother had left the Hudson Ranch—likely hot-wired her car, since Jack doubted she'd left her keys behind—and was quite clearly up to no good.

Jack could tell she was looking straight ahead, staring hard at her car parked there. Jack couldn't make out her expression in just the glow of the flashlight, but he could feel the hurt radiating off her.

She audibly swallowed. "I'm calling Detective Delaney-Carson," she whispered, reaching for her pocket.

Jack put his hand over hers before she could grab her phone. "We can handle this, Chloe. You don't have to call it in if you don't want to."

She finally turned to look at him. He couldn't make out her features in the dark. She was just a shadow, but her voice was convincing enough. Firm and determined. "Yes. Yes, I do."

CHLOE'S HAND SHOOK as she held the phone to her ear, but she didn't think Jack saw the tremor. He was busy watching all around them, making sure they weren't sitting ducks.

For what, she didn't know. Whatever was going on... nothing added up or made any sense. But she could feel danger in the air like an impending storm.

There wasn't any movement from the car. No sounds but the rustles and chirps of an evening in the wilderness. Wherever Ry was, it wasn't right here. Chloe refused to let her mind bound ahead to worst-case scenarios. Most likely, he was out here scoring a hit from some drug dealer.

Funny how she *hoped* that was all it was.

The phone rang and when the detective answered, it was with a terse, "Yes."

"It's Deputy Brink. We haven't found any sign of Hart, but my brother took off from the Hudson Ranch. We've tracked him to a parking lot in the Franklin Forest. I don't know if it connects to Hart, to the scrapbook, but I think you should send someone over. We've found my car that he used, abandoned in a lot."

There was a pause. "I'm coming myself," she replied. "We got word from Texas. Mark Brink didn't show up for his last parole meeting. He's missing."

Chloe didn't swear. She couldn't even muster up surprise. Maybe she didn't think her father was behind stealing that scrapbook because it didn't make any sense, but maybe she was giving him too much credit to think he *had* to make sense.

"I'll send you our exact location," Chloe said.

"Good. I'll be there soon."

The call ended, and Chloe sent the location to Delaney-Carson. She took a deep breath, staring at her car. Parked. Ry's phone must be in the car, but Ry wasn't.

Unless...

She swallowed down a bubble of fear. If he was hurt, well, she'd deal with it. "Let's look at the car but not touch anything. I don't want anyone accusing us of tampering." Because if she stood here waiting for Laurel without doing anything, she'd think of a million terrible situations that involved Ry bloody and dead somewhere and she couldn't...

She was so angry at him, but she knew herself well enough to know she'd make a wrong choice if she let herself get too worked up about the possibilities of him being hurt. And she... She'd made too many bad choices when it came to her brother.

That ended now.

"Chloe—"

"If I say we should look at it, we should look at it. If you want to go first and keep me behind you, I'd start moving." She knew she was being a jerk when Jack was trying to be protective and sweet, in his way, but she was holding on by a thread.

She needed to do everything she could to treat this like a crime scene that had nothing to do with her. To treat Jack like a fellow cop, not the man she loved.

They moved forward in tandem, Chloe training the flashlight on the car. They were quiet, watching for movement, listening for sound. But there was nothing as they got close enough to the car to look inside.

Chloe swept the beam over the entire car and in each window, heart in her throat, *praying* it would be empty.

And it was. There was nothing amiss inside. It looked almost exactly like it had when she'd left it on the Hudson Ranch, with the one exception of Ry's phone lying in the console.

That made her nervous, of course, but at least it wasn't a body.

At this point, Ry had made bad choices. She could accept that. She had given him every opportunity to make different, better choices. He'd refused. She could mourn that, but she couldn't keep blaming herself for it.

But she could never stop hoping he was alive. Hoping he'd find some way to get himself out of all the choices he'd made. Maybe it hurt her heart, but that was the bottom line now.

Meanwhile, Jack Hudson stood beside her, offering *not* to call the authorities they needed to call, wanting to protect her—and if that meant bending his very strict moral code, apparently he was willing to do it.

Chloe couldn't let him. It would just about kill her.

"I want to know who he talked to, but we better wait for Bent County to open the door with gloves. There might be prints that give us a hint as to what's going on. If he was here with someone else." She looked out into the darkness around them. "Meeting someone? I don't know. But it's going to be Bent County's job to figure it out."

Jack nodded. "Okay, but if he drove your car here, left it here, we should be able to pick up his trail for a little while." Jack reached for the flashlight. He didn't take it from her but pushed it down a little so the light illuminated their footprints. Nothing super clear, but enough of an indentation to tell that someone had been walking across the makeshift lot. "Or we can stay here and wait."

It was up to her. A lump formed in her throat. Funny how she wouldn't mind him sweeping in and making the decisions for her right now. But that was because these were the kind of decisions she had to make for herself, even if she didn't want to.

Chloe used the beam, searching out footprints that weren't hers or Jack's. Eventually she zeroed in on a pair that was either Ry's or some other random person's. Jack walked ahead, gun drawn and at the ready, as her beam led them away from the parking lot and into the low grasses that made up the field in front of them. There was a path, it looked like, though it was hard to tell in only the beam of the flashlight if it was just from animals trampling through or an actual marked hiking trail in the forest.

She didn't want to follow his footsteps too far with Bent County coming, but it was hard to hold herself back knowing Ry could be out there. Doing who knew what.

"Chloe."

Jack had that tone in his voice. Like something bad was coming, but she didn't see what it could be. She looked around, she listened, but nothing.

Then his hand came over her wrist, he pulled her a little forward and he moved the light beam to something on the ground.

It was just a small little circle, but Chloe had been a cop too long not to know what blood dropped onto dirt looked like.

Her hand shook for a second, but only a second. The

light trembling was enough for her to ground herself. To remind herself she was strong, capable. A *cop*, not a big sister who'd failed.

She moved the beam up the trail. Not much farther up, there was another spot, about the same size as the first.

She took a few steps forward, and Jack never released her hand, but he didn't stop her. He moved with her.

The third circle was bigger. Noticeably so. She inhaled, knowing it was shaky. Knowing she couldn't quite make herself immune to this.

Someone was bleeding, and the chances it *wasn't* Ry felt really, really low.

"What do you want to do?" Jack asked her quietly. "Wait or follow?"

They should wait. That would be the safe thing to do. But as much as she was ready for her brother to face the consequences of his actions, she wasn't ready for him to be hurt. Or worse, dead.

"Follow."

Chapter Fifteen

Jack walked in front of Chloe, following the lead of the flashlight she held. Every few steps, there was a splotch of blood. Sometimes they got smaller, but then they'd get bigger again.

Jack gripped his gun. He occasionally looked out into the dark around them but never caught sight of anything, never heard anything that seemed out of place. Even though he was on edge, there wasn't that feeling of impending danger to him and Chloe.

But there had been danger here, that was for sure. The blood splotches along the trail no longer got smaller, only bigger, until they became almost a continuous trickle of blood.

Every so often, Jack glanced back at Chloe holding the flashlight. He could feel the tension pouring off her. She was worried it was Ry doing the bleeding, and so was Jack. The other option wasn't much better—that Ry had been the person to cause the bleeding in someone else. Both were going to be hard pills to swallow for Chloe. But there was no pill to swallow until they figured out what was going on here.

Jack wondered how long they could walk before they found something, before Bent County arrived at the parking lot and wondered where they were. He wondered a lot of things on this slow, nerve-racking walk that never seemed to end.

The trail narrowed, and the trickle of blood seemed to disappear. Though, more likely, whatever had been bleeding was now bleeding in the grass rather than the dirt.

Jack paused, not sure whether to press on or study the grassy sides of the trail for the blood. No doubt it didn't just miraculously stop bleeding.

"Jack." Her voice trembled on just the single syllable of his name.

He heard it then. The rustle and clicking sounds. Not a human threat, but animal. Still, he wasn't sure why that would scare Chloe, who'd grown up around wildlife and the potential threat and danger of them just as much as he had.

Until he turned to where the beam was pointed. Two pairs of eyes glowed back at them. But it wasn't the animals— coyotes—that had caused that reaction in Chloe. It was what they were standing next to.

A human body.

Jack moved without fully thinking. Just placed himself between her and the body. Just made sure his body stopped the beam of light from reaching that far. He hadn't seen the details, just the body—the very still body—being studied and perhaps other things by the coyotes.

"It's Ry, isn't it? It's... He... Someone..."

Jack moved forward and pulled her into him. "We don't know that, Chloe."

Her breathing hitched on a little sob. "It's *someone*."

He wanted to give her his gun and tell her to follow the trail back to the parking lot. Wait for the cops. He wanted her to let him handle whatever this was. But it would leave him with only his phone for a light and with no other form of protection. He didn't think the coyotes would be much of a problem if he didn't approach, but he'd have to approach to identify the body.

Chloe needed to know. For sure. So he couldn't send her back yet. He had to...

"Stay here. Put your phone flashlight on, and give me this one." He pried the flashlight from her fingers. He didn't think she was holding it so tight because she didn't want to relinquish control, but because she was in shock.

"Chloe," he said sharply. She jerked her gaze to him. "Pull out your phone. I'm going to get closer and see if I can get an ID."

She shook her head. "Jack, they'll... You can't approach wild animals feeding."

"I'll be careful. You stand right here."

"Jack."

But he ignored her protests and moved forward. Luckily, she stayed put, or he would have had to stop. He didn't want her seeing whatever this was, but he knew she needed answers.

He'd get her those answers.

He pointed the beam back at the animals. They didn't move, but they watched him approach. Then they started to move a little nervously. Low growls began to emanate from where they stood.

Jack made a few ridiculous noises, loud and sudden, hoping to scare the coyotes off as he approached. They were clearly reluctant to leave the body, and reluctant to deal with Jack. They backed off a *little*, though not as far away as Jack would have preferred.

He moved the beam from the coyotes to the body. An

arm was bloody and mangled, no doubt some from the coyotes, but perhaps some from whatever injury had caused the trail of blood, because most of the body looked to be intact.

Jack circled, hoping to get closer to the head and face. As he did, he saw hair, and immediately knew it wasn't Ry because the brown was too long and peppered with gray.

"Chloe, it's not Ry," he called out to her, still trying to creep close enough to get a glimpse of the face without upsetting the coyotes too much. He kept making noises and flashing the beam of the flashlight at the animals, hoping to keep them back.

They did keep inching away, but they didn't stop their warning growls or take off like he might have preferred. Still, he got to a better angle, slightly closer, and was able to point the light at the face of the body.

Not Ry. Familiar, but Jack wasn't sure… Until it dawned on him just who it was.

He let out a slow breath, then began to back away from the body, from the coyotes, back toward Chloe.

When he reached her, he realized she was shaking. She hadn't turned the light on her phone on, but she held it in her hands.

"Chloe."

"It's Ry, isn't it? It has to be. It's the only thing that makes sense." She was crying. Panicking, clearly.

He had his hands full and wasn't quite sure whether to put down the light or the gun. In the end, he placed the flashlight on the ground and gripped her arm with his free one. "Chloe, listen to me, sweetheart. It's not Ry."

She nodded, like him touching her finally got it through to her. When she finally spoke, her words were choked. "Then who is it, Jack?"

He took a deep breath. He didn't want to draw it out, and still… It was hard to say. "It's your father."

CHLOE DIDN'T BREAK DOWN. Or at least, she didn't lose it over the fact her father was dead. That information kind of helped her pull herself together. Breathe again, wipe her cheeks. In those first few moments, she couldn't have cared less about her dead father. She had just been so damn relieved her brother hadn't ended up that way.

So far.

Then the chaos had started, which was kind of a nice distraction. It was this strange, buzzing foundation to whatever was going on inside her. Jack took her back to the parking lot, where Detective Delaney-Carson had arrived and was investigating the car.

Jack told the detective everything—or at least, Chloe thought he had. The panic that it had been Ry lying in a bloody, dead heap had been hard to fully come out of. And the fact of the matter was, even knowing it *wasn't* Ry didn't ease her worry. Because Ry was still out there somewhere since this was her car in the parking lot.

Maybe Ry was the aggressor, but more likely to Chloe's way of thinking, he was another victim to whatever their father had dragged him into.

Detective Delaney-Carson called in more backup, and pretty soon there were cops everywhere. Dealing with the coyotes and the body, and determining what their next steps were going to be.

Jack had tried to convince Chloe to go back to the Hudson Ranch multiple times, and even the detective had suggested it, but Chloe couldn't budge. Not until they found Ry.

She kept expecting to feel something when they brought

her father's body out of that field in a body bag. Some sort of...not grief, obviously, when he'd been nothing to her, really, besides a tormenter. But she'd expected to feel *something.*

Instead, there was nothing but an odd sort of numbness when it came to her father's death. Murder. Whatever it was. The only feeling she really recognized was worry over Ry, over whatever was going on with Hart missing, about what this all meant for Jack's family. Really, about what this all *meant.*

Because as much as she'd felt her father didn't have anything to do with stealing that scrapbook, there were no leads here. No answers. Just a dead man. So it was more questions and no leads.

"Deputy Brink, I'd like to ask you a few questions."

"I think any questions can wait," Jack said, stepping in between the detective and Chloe herself.

It was funny how she could appreciate the gesture but not want it all the same. "No, I'd like to answer all the questions I can right now. I want my brother found. No matter what."

Jack moved to the side, still standing beside her but no longer blocking the detective, and it was the combination of sticking up for her and being able to stand aside that gave her the ability to lean on him, when she usually didn't want to lean on anyone.

"Do you have any reason to believe your brother could have killed your father?" the detective asked.

Chloe let that question settle over her. It was the natural one to ask, and it was one she'd been asking herself since Jack had broken the news to her. "My father was a cruel man. He was verbally, emotionally and physically abusive toward Ry. But in the way of abusers, Ry might have spoken badly about him, he might have even hated him, but he did what my father told him to do. Is it *possible* Ry had a moment of snapping? Of finally refusing and that resulted in some kind of altercation that left my father dead? Sure, it's possible. Is it plausible? No. Because he's still an immature boy seeking the wrong people's approval."

And he was out there. Somewhere. Probably in this forest preserve. And maybe her brother was capable of murder. Maybe that was in him, and she was blind to it. Maybe her father had pushed and pushed, threatened, started it. Maybe Ry had finished it and panicked. Possible. So possible.

And yet she just couldn't visualize it. She couldn't buy into it. Not with Hart and that scrapbook missing. There was some thread they were missing. Eventually, the detectives would find it, and normally she would step back and let them.

But she couldn't do that with Ry missing.

"Deputy Brink, I'm going to ask you to go home," the detective said. "Or to the Hudson Ranch. I'm going to ask you to leave this up to Bent County to investigate."

"Are you going to expect me to listen?"

There was a pause. The detective looked at the scene around them. Flashlights and cops and a vast wilderness that could hide so many answers. Then her gaze returned to Chloe, and she shook her head. "No, I'm not."

"Good."

"Just try to stay out of my guys' way. And keep me in the loop. I think the timing is too coincidental. I don't know how it doesn't connect, but if Hart and that scrapbook have nothing to do with your brother and father, that means we've got two cases to solve instead of one. I need your cooperation."

Before, Chloe might have hesitated, being worried about Ry and trouble. But they were in the same position, really. The detective's partner was missing, someone she probably cared about from years of working together. Someone she was responsible for due to the nature of their jobs. Chloe's brother was missing, and she loved the little rat bastard.

Connected or not, they were problems that needed solving no matter what. So they'd have to work together. "You've got it."

Someone hailed the detective, and she excused herself. Chloe turned to Jack and took a deep breath. She met his gaze—not cop-blank but worried. About her.

"I'm going to ask you to go home, Jack."

"Chloe—"

"Hear me out. This is… This place has meaning to you. Bad meaning. You shouldn't have to scour it and be reminded. You can send Baker or Clinton out to help me. I can ask Carlyle to come out—she's got the skills to help me look for Ry. Or even Zeke would probably help. It doesn't have to be you *here*."

"It doesn't have to be, no. But it's going to be."

She'd known that was going to be his answer. She'd known she wouldn't be able to talk him into leaving. And still, she'd needed to hear him say it. To get that stern, irritable look from him at her even suggesting he left her to this.

"I love you, Jack." And who the hell cared if there were cops all around them. She loved him, and no matter what horrible things were happening, they were going to make this one thing work.

She was determined.

Chapter Sixteen

Jack didn't bother to try to convince Chloe to go home and rest and eat first, though he wanted to. It would be the smart thing to do. He knew this rationally.

But he'd also been in her position before. He knew too well what it felt like to have a family member in danger. There'd be no rest, no taking care of herself, until they'd exhausted every resource in finding Ry.

Because it was one thing for Ry to be missing, running off on his own volition, but to be missing with one body already found was something else. Something urgent.

But where to begin? The cops were crawling all over the parking lot and crime scene, gathering clues, compiling evidence. Of course, their focus was on a dead Mark Brink and a missing detective, not Ry. Not yet. Not when they had one of their own missing.

"What if we follow that trail past where my father was found?" Chloe suggested. "Ry didn't come back to the car, and I'm not sure I buy that he and my father were out here if they weren't together. Especially with *my* car. Ry had to go somewhere. Somewhere in the preserve."

Jack didn't want to burst her bubble, but they had to analyze all the facts. "Your father might have had a vehicle. Ry could have taken that." Or been taken *in* that, though

Jack didn't point it out. Maybe they didn't need to analyze *every* possibility. "Whoever killed your father could have had a vehicle."

"Did you see evidence of anyone else?" Chloe returned.

He hadn't, though, in fairness, it was hard to determine what was wind mark and what was made by car and human in the dirt of the parking area. It wasn't an often-visited area since the campground was on the other side of the preserve. You'd have to be a pretty intrepid hiker to be on this side. So a lack of evidence of other people *could* point to something.

He supposed it was just as possible Ry was still in the preserve as not. But it was a *vast* preserve. "I'm not sure even with Laurel's okay they're going to let us walk down that trail again."

"Let's go around and meet it up a ways after." Chloe looked down at her phone screen and the map of the forest preserve she'd pulled up. "If we walk back to the road, then take it a while, we can cut over. Should be light by then, and we'll have an easier time of meeting up with the trail from the road."

Jack wasn't sure it was the best idea, but he knew Chloe needed to feel like she had a handle on something. Besides, even if it was the wrong avenue to go down, the entire Bent County Sheriff's Department was also looking into this whole thing. They could stumble into finding Ry as well.

Hopefully alive. Hopefully not a murderer.

But first, he had to be found, so Jack nodded at Chloe, and they started walking back out to the road. There was a hint of a sunrise to the east. She was right: it wouldn't take long for the light to catch up with them.

That would be good. That would help. Jack told himself

this over and over again. That he was the sheriff, that this was his *job*. Not a painful tightrope walk with the woman he loved, trying to unearth secrets that would hurt them both.

"Losing service," Chloe muttered, holding her phone up to the sky as if that might help. "I don't think we should cross over to the trail just yet. We need to go at least another half mile." She lifted her hand, poked at something on one of those high-tech watches Jack couldn't begin to understand.

"You know, you should get one, Jack," she said, as if she'd read his mind.

"I don't even like my cell phone. Why would I want it on my wrist?"

She shook her head, her mouth curving ever so slightly. The old, familiar argument was something like a comfort in the middle of all this unfamiliar.

"Do you know where it was?" she asked, not looking at him as they walked.

He didn't have to be a mind reader to understand what she was asking. "The campground on the north side was the last place anyone saw them. I've been up and down every inch of it, and this preserve. We're pretty far away."

She nodded. "Ry was too young to have been involved in that, but… Maybe we should head that way after we follow the trail for a bit. I don't think any of these things make sense enough to connect, except for the timing. I want to ignore the timing, I really do, because it feels so circumstantial. But…"

"Timing is part of it. I agree. We'll head out that way if the trail doesn't offer anything."

This time, she did look over at him. "Another thing you don't have to be here for."

"I'll be here," he said, and realized she had said the same exact thing, at the same exact time, mimicking his deep voice while she did it.

He frowned at her, but there was no heat behind it. In truth, he was glad she could still make fun of him in the midst of this mess.

Still, he wanted to make sure she understood. "Not leaving your side, Chloe."

She reached out with her free hand, laced her fingers with his. "Thanks."

They walked, hand in hand, in silence for the rest of the way until her watch beeped, signaling they'd walked far enough to cut through the low-level brush and find the trail.

The world was all alight now, still pearly and dim, but they wouldn't be risking twisting an ankle or stepping on something that didn't want to be stepped on by heading off-road to cut toward the trail.

They'd taken only a step or two off the road when they both paused. Jack thought he'd heard something from behind them. Likely from the parking lot, where even now a couple of Bent County deputies were working; though that wasn't the direction the sound had *seemed* to come from.

But in their stillness, Jack heard it again. A noise. A human noise. From the opposite direction of the parking lot. It had to have been.

Because it was someone's voice. And whatever they'd said sounded a lot like *help*. The cops certainly wouldn't be yelling for help.

"Is that someone calling for help?" Chloe asked, her hand squeezing tight in his. Too hopeful, too desperate for it to be Ry.

So he held her still to keep her from immediately running toward it and hated having to be the voice of reason. "Sounds like it—but we need to be careful, Chloe. We don't know what we're dealing with. Calls for help are just as likely tricks to—"

"I know, Jack," she said, but she was already moving toward the noise. Though she didn't pull out of his grasp, just pulled him along with her. Back onto the road and farther up.

He could have stopped her, but he didn't have the heart. They'd approach carefully. Together. They'd protect each other.

Jack realized they were close to the edge of the preserve that backed up to the highway. It could have been a trick of noise carrying. It could have been...

But as they walked around a curve in the road, they both spotted someone. Jack put his free hand on the butt of his weapon as he scanned the area. One solitary figure. Stumbling.

Too tall to be Ry, but there didn't appear to be a weapon, a threat. Still, Jack didn't take his hand off his gun until...

Both he and Chloe seemed to recognize the man at the same time, because they said his name and moved forward at a jog in unison.

When they reached Hart, he stumbled a little when he lifted his head to look at them. It was clear he'd been hurt. Blood crusted over the side of his face. But he was alive, and that was better than Mark Brink.

It wasn't Ry, and that was a shame for Chloe, but maybe it was a lead. If all these disparate things connected.

"Hart, what the hell happened?" Jack asked, dropping his hand off his gun and offering an arm for the man to lean against him. The fact that Hart did gave way to just how hurt he was.

"It was a woman," he rasped. Jack couldn't make sense of the words right away.

"A woman?" Chloe repeated gently. She stood on the other side of him, ready to take any other needed weight.

"I was getting into my car at the sheriff's department, and I heard a woman scream for help," Hart said, clearly trying to find the strength to stand on his own two feet as he recounted what had happened. "I looked over and I saw her. So I jogged over. I think I did...? I don't know. It's a little fuzzy. The next thing I really remember is waking up. Which I did, because I fell." He gestured with one arm, hissed out a breath, clearly in pain. "Not sure where I was. I think I might have been dumped out of the back of a truck. Once I could, I got up and started walking, hoping to find someone."

That would make sense, as they were close to the highway out here. Jack surveyed the distance between where they were and the parking lot where the other Bent County deputies were. Too far.

"We'll call you an ambulance," Jack said.

"Call Laurel. She'll get it sorted and know I'm okay all in one fell swoop, and she can pass it around to my family."

Chloe nodded and pulled her phone out of her pocket, taking a few steps away—in search of service, no doubt.

"I don't know what the hell's going on, Sheriff," Hart said in a quiet tone Chloe wouldn't be able to hear. "But I do know whatever it is ties to the Brink family. There's just no way it doesn't."

CHLOE JOGGED AWAY in search of service. Jack and Hart followed at a slower pace, and when she finally had a bar, she lifted her phone to her ear and called Detective Delaney-Carson.

She tried to feel relief as they moved through the next steps. A sense of happiness that even though Hart was hurt, he hadn't ended up like her father.

But Ry was somewhere out there, and she wasn't sure she'd feel anything good until she knew where. Until she knew he was okay.

With the phone call made, Chloe fell back into step with Jack and Hart. Chloe wondered if they should have him sit and rest, but if he'd suffered any kind of concussion, he probably needed to stay alert.

"What did this woman who called for help look like?" Jack asked Hart.

Hart licked cracked lips. He needed water. Probably some stitches for that gash on his head. They should really let him take it easy, but Chloe wanted answers, so she didn't stop Jack's questions.

"I don't really remember. It happened so fast. I heard it more than anything. 'Help.' Someone needed help." He said it as if trying to convince himself when it was clear that it had been a ploy. A ploy to get him away from the scrapbook, and that had to have been perpetrated by more than one person.

And none of those people could have been her dead father. He hadn't had the scrapbook on his corpse.

Ry also couldn't be involved in that. Because Hart had disappeared *before* Ry had taken off from the ranch. So he wasn't involved. She tried to comfort herself with that knowledge.

But she was too much of a cop not to accept that while he hadn't been part of the ploy to distract or hurt Hart, that still didn't mean he couldn't be involved in other things that connected.

Some comfort.

"I didn't have my full belt on me, but I did have my gun. They took it," Hart said with disgust. He stumbled a little, even with Jack holding him up, so they stopped their progress.

Chloe knew she shouldn't keep poking at him. He was hurt. But… "They also took the scrapbook. Out of your car. From the security footage, it seems like that's what they were after. Them letting you go seems to add credence to that theory."

Hart scowled. His gaze lifted briefly to Chloe, but then he looked back at Jack. He didn't say anything to that, so Chloe continued.

"You guys looked through the scrapbook when you had it. Right? You looked through it and couldn't find any evidence of note. But Delaney-Carson said she thought you should keep it, and you were the one who wanted to give it back."

"She wanted your take on it," Hart confirmed.

"So, what was in it?" Jack asked.

"It was black-and-white pictures. Old people. Ranches. Homesteader stuff with plat maps. Boring. Pointless." He glanced at Chloe again. And even though she could see suspicion in his gaze, she couldn't get mad at a man with a bloody face who couldn't even walk without help right now.

"I figured if it connected to what's going on, you'd lead us to whatever connection once you had it."

Then she realized what Hart's plan had *really* been. "You were going to follow me." It shouldn't make her angry. It was decent enough police work.

But it was barking up the wrong tree, so she couldn't quite ignore the feelings of frustration bubbling up inside her.

"I was going to investigate," Hart said coolly.

By following me. But she supposed she didn't need to argue with an injured man. It didn't change anything. He'd been hurt, the scrapbook had been taken and she didn't have the first clue as to *why.*

"Did you ever see the woman who called for help? Stranger? Maybe someone familiar?" Jack pressed.

Hart took some time to think about it. "I'm not really sure. I think... There had to have been two of them, right? If I went to help the woman, someone had to jump me from behind." He gestured at the bloody portion of his head.

True. And either one could have been the person in the hoodie who'd come back and taken the scrapbook. But there also could have been a third. Too many people involved now. What kind of sense did that make?

The ambulance finally came and so did Detective Delaney-Carson, relief etched in every line of her face. She explained that she'd called his family, asked him a few questions and then instructed the ambulance to take him away.

Laurel watched the ambulance go, then turned to face them both. Her expression was grim, her words all warning.

"We're dealing with two attackers—that we know of, there could have been more. These could be our murderers, or there could be more. I'm going to go to the hospital in a bit so I can ask him some more questions once he's been fully checked out. I know you guys want answers just as much as I do, but I wouldn't recommend heading out into this isolated place just the two of you. That's begging for trouble."

When neither Jack nor Chloe said anything, she sighed. Then she opened the bag she was carrying. She pulled out a couple of granola bars and two water bottles.

"This won't do much, and I'd recommend a full meal and some sleep, but you're not going to listen, so..." she said as they took the offered sustenance. "I have to focus on my investigation, my guys. Understand the risks before you go wading into it."

Chloe nodded and glanced at Jack, who was doing the same.

"I'll leave you to it then. Watch your backs. I'll try to contact you when we get some answers, but if you go out there, it'll be hard to reach you."

Again, silence seemed to be the best response, so Chloe kept her mouth shut and so did Jack.

Laurel shook her head. "It's a bad idea, guys."

But she turned and left them to it without any further warnings.

Chloe wasn't sure what their next move was going to be, but she'd search every inch of this forest preserve to find Ry. And she couldn't possibly go home and rest or eat before she did.

"She's right," Jack said once Laurel was gone.

Chloe turned to face him, her stomach sinking. Because she couldn't go back to the ranch and just wait. She *couldn't*. She knew he wouldn't leave her to handle this alone, but she couldn't possibly let him bulldoze her into going back to the ranch. "Jack—"

"Just the two of us *is* begging for trouble," he said firmly. Then his gaze moved from the horizon to meet hers. "So let's call in reinforcements."

Chapter Seventeen

A little over an hour later, they had a group of Hudsons and Daniels huddled together in the morning sun at the center of the forest preserve. Zeke, Carlyle, Grant, Hawk, Anna and Palmer had all come out. Louisa would join them later, after she was done working at her parents' orchard, if it took that long.

Because this was what family did. Jack had spent a lot of years considering himself the solitary, lone leader. The person who had to keep it all together without leaning too hard on anyone else for help. He'd spent a lot of time and energy trying to protect his siblings from pain, danger, risk.

Of course, he'd always had help, particularly from Mary and Grant in those early years, but he'd also made sure most of the responsibility lay on his shoulders. Or tried to.

If there was anything the past few years had taught him, it was that he didn't need to do that anymore. It had been hard to let go of all the responsibility he felt had defined him, but he thought he was finally really getting there. His siblings' lives the past few years certainly hadn't given him much choice.

Still, he hated asking for help. But for Chloe? He'd ask anyone. Because she was part of it too. She'd given him some hope for a future, even if he worried how well he'd be able to give her what she deserved.

But for right now, they had to find her brother.

He explained the entire situation to everyone who'd come, and Carlyle and Anna flanked Chloe like two sentries ready and willing to fight for her.

Because she wasn't alone, and she wasn't going to be. None of them would let her be. He hoped she was beginning to understand she didn't have to take it all on her shoulders herself too.

Grant had had the presence of mind to bring a paper map they could spread out and all look at to determine how they'd approach the search.

"Chloe and I will take the campground," Jack said, pointing to it on the map. He met Chloe's gaze because she'd opened her mouth to argue, but one sharp look from him and she closed it. He wasn't going to repeat himself about being by her side. It was a done deal.

"We'll approach from the south end. Zeke and Carlyle, I'd like you guys to come at it from the north." Because Zeke and Carlyle hadn't come into the Hudson orbit until long after their parents were gone, so they shouldn't have any emotional connection to the campsite. He'd send his siblings off into other corners and hope that it wasn't a mistake.

"Can I beat him up if I find him first?" Carlyle asked darkly, holding a grudge against Ry for sneaking away on her watch.

"With my permission," Chloe returned vehemently.

Jack could see she was trying to hold on to a kind of tough outer demeanor, and maybe it would have been better for Chloe if he'd paired her up with Carlyle. Maybe it was selfish to want to keep her in his sight, by his side.

Well, so be it.

As for his siblings, he paired them up and gave them their assignments. Anna argued with him about a few minor details, because of course she did, but when Chloe took his side, Anna backed off.

"Most of us won't have cell service as we move deeper into the preserve, but everybody has a flare, right?" Everyone nodded. Palmer had brought packs that would keep them going for a while, provided everyone with water and a weapon as well as a flare. They could feasibly spend the rest of daylight hours out here searching.

Jack hoped it wouldn't come to that.

"No matter what, everyone meets back here at four. No exceptions."

Everyone murmured their assent, then began to pair off into vehicles that would lead them to their different corners. They'd go to their assigned areas, canvass on foot for a few hours, then meet back here in the middle of the preserve.

Hopefully, with a safe-and-sound Ry Brink in tow.

Jack climbed into the driver's seat of his truck, waited for Chloe to get into the passenger side. They said nothing. Jack just drove through the twists and turns of paved roads, then gravel ones, until they approached the campground.

Tension seeped into him. If those skeletal remains on the Brink Ranch were his parents, there was nothing about this place that should make him tense, that should make dread and grief settle deep in his gut. Because if they'd been buried elsewhere, there was likely no remnants of what had happened to them *here*.

And yet no matter what he *thought*, what he knew, the

feelings were twisting around inside him as they got out of the truck at the entrance to the campground. He shouldered the pack Palmer had brought for him and tried to shake away his unease as he scanned the area.

On this side of the preserve, spruce trees towered and reached for a bright blue sky. It dappled the campground in dark shadows in direct contrast to the sunny day. At the front of the truck, Chloe reached out and took his hand.

None of his inner scolding had settled the anxiety he felt, but her hand in his did. It didn't take it all away, but it soothed some of those jagged feelings. They were in this together, whatever the answers might be.

They moved forward in unison, not quite sure what they were looking for. Signs of life. Signs of Ry. *Signs.*

The campground had some tents and some campers. Definitely not as deserted as other areas of the park. So he and Chloe walked down the little campground road, eyeing each campsite for anything that might stand out.

There was an older couple huddled around a campfire, putting together some kind of lunch. Jack didn't realize he'd stopped walking until Chloe gently tugged at his hand. He looked away from the couple and toward the road. He couldn't bear to look at Chloe and see sympathy on her face.

It didn't do him any good to think that his parents might be doing just that if they'd lived. They hadn't, and he had to focus on the living. But Chloe let go of his hand, tucked her arm around his waist so they were walking hip to hip.

He managed a slow, big breath that loosened the tightness in his chest. Focus on the living, on the future. On the task at hand. Which all centered on her.

They reached the end of the campsite road. Carlyle and Zeke would be catching up to them soon unless something had happened. Both Jack and Chloe looked around. Then Chloe pointed at a little outhouse. "There's a trail there. Are there more campsites that way?"

"Usually not when the campgrounds have empty sites closer to the facilities, but let's go check."

They moved past the outhouse, onto a trail that led to overflow campsites. Jack didn't see any tents set up along the trail, but as he and Chloe began to move, he heard someone. Just the whisper of a word, like a curse under someone's breath. And then the heavy, pounding footsteps of someone running.

Away.

Jack swore himself, turning to see someone's quickly retreating form.

Not just *someone*. Ry.

So Jack took off after him.

CHLOE WANTED TO cry with relief, and at the very same time, she wanted to beat her brother up. Tears threatened, but luckily, running as hard as she could through the forest helped keep them from leaking out.

If Ry was running, it was bad in that he was probably mixed up in a hell of a lot of trouble. Because he had to have seen it was them, so he wasn't in the kind of trouble he wanted help with.

But he was *running*. So he was alive and whole, and no matter how angry she was at him, relief lightened all her harsher emotions.

She was going to *figuratively* kill the little bastard. Right after she hugged him so tight, she was sure he was okay.

Jack had longer legs and could move faster for short-term distances, but Chloe had a better stride for longer distances and, because of her smaller size, was able to dodge trees with more agility, so after a bit of running, she bypassed Jack and was quickly gaining on her brother.

"Rylan Jonas Brink, stop running right now!"

He didn't listen, though he looked back over his shoulder. Tactical mistake, because after a couple more steps, he tripped and then went sprawling. Giving Chloe just enough time to catch up to him and pounce.

He struggled under her tackle, trying to buck her off. "I didn't do anything!"

She got her knee in his back, managed to wrench one arm behind him even as her breath sawed in and out. "Then why are you running?" She resisted punching him though she itched to, even as she was desperate to hug him and hold him tight. Alive, *alive*.

And in so much damn trouble.

"Let me," Jack said beside her. She realized he was holding handcuffs, and she sighed. She adjusted her hold so Jack could do the honors.

Though she wouldn't have minded cuffing her brother herself in this moment.

Jack secured Ry's hands behind his back and dragged him back a few feet so that he was in a sitting position and could lean against a tree trunk.

Ry's gaze moved back and forth, from Jack to Chloe, then beyond them as if he was looking for someone to come rescue him. Or maybe take him away.

"What are you guys doing here?" Ry demanded, falling back on being surly and accusatory. Because why wouldn't he, cuffed and outnumbered?

She really hoped whatever he'd gotten himself mixed up with, whatever punishments ended up being doled out, would get through his thick skull and make him realize he could be so much more than he allowed himself to be.

"What are *we* doing here?" Chloe said, barely resisting a sneer. "You snuck away from the Hudsons. You *stole* my car. What the hell do you think we're doing here?"

"I'm just borrowing it! Why do you always have to over-react?"

Chloe had often wondered if her brother would give her an aneurysm, but this really took the cake. She took a deep breath, trying to resist the urge to scream at him.

"Why did you take my car to that parking lot, leave your phone in it and end up all the way over here?" Jack asked, his voice low and calm. Clearly trying to de-escalate the situation.

Chloe didn't know if that was possible. "And how?" she added darkly.

"I don't—"

"Don't lie to me." She pointed her finger at him, narrowly resisted poking him. Hard. "Do you know what kind of trouble you're in right now? Tell the damn truth, Ry."

Ry rolled his eyes, and she would have reached out and punched him, probably, but Jack put a hand on her arm. She swallowed down the suddenly swirling anger. Or tried to.

She didn't know how to get through Ry's thick head, and he was making it impossible to feel any kind of sorry for him.

"You'll just get ticked off, but there's nothing to get mad about," Ry said, in his usual defiant, oh-so-victimized way. "Dad wanted to meet up. He's on parole, so it'd have to be quick so he could get back to Texas. I knew it'd get back to you if I did it anywhere where people could see, so we agreed to meet here. I drove over and I waited for him, and he didn't show. I knew you'd start looking for me, so I figured I'd just walk around for a bit."

It was a lie—or at least, partly a lie. She doubted very much Ry had walked all the way from the parking lot to this campground. Maybe it was *possible* in the hours that had passed, but he didn't look like he'd done any major walking or hiking.

Granted, it didn't look like he'd killed anyone, either, but she didn't know what to think about his ability to do that anymore. So she told him. Flat out.

She knelt next to him, looked him straight in the eye. Not because she wanted to soften the blow, whatever blow it would be, but because she wanted to watch every last inch of his reaction. "Dad's dead, Ry."

She watched as Ry's expression drooped and his entire face blanched. There was no shifty discomfort, no guilt, just straight-up shock. "Dead? He shouldn't be…" Ry swallowed. "You saw him? Dead? You're sure he's dead?"

"Yes."

"But…" Ry shook his head. He looked up at Jack, then back at Chloe right in front of him. Some little war played out over his expression, but she had seen Ry guilty enough times to know none of it was guilt. She'd seen him lie enough times to know what he was working through wasn't a lie.

"Chloe, you have to get out of here." He said it seriously, urgently, leaning forward. "I've got it handled, okay? But you've got to go. She'll…"

She? It made Chloe think of what Hart had said: a woman had called for help. A woman was involved. Did this connect to Hart more than their father? But Ry didn't say anything, just trailed off.

So she leaned forward too, got in his face. "Who, Ry?"

He shook his head vehemently, his eyes wide and worried. "I can't tell you, Chlo. Please. *Please.* Save yourself. Just let me go. There's no way it works out if you don't get out of here. Fast." He was so earnest, and yes, Ry was a good liar when he wanted to be, but she saw something like genuine fear in his gaze.

Like he actually was trying to protect her. She leaned back a little, his fear sparking her own. Ry trying to be noble felt more worrisome than anything else that had happened today.

She reached out, gripped his shoulder tightly. Hoping some kind of connection would get through all...whatever this was. There was always this wall between them, and she needed to scale it. His attitude, his refusals. Hurdles he refused to acknowledge. But she had to get through to him somehow. "You need to be straight with me. For once. Damn it, Ry. For once, tell me what the hell is going on."

He leaned forward, so close that their noses were almost touching while she held on to his shoulder. When he spoke, he enunciated each word clearly, his eyes a maze of fear and determination she'd never seen in him before.

"I can't tell you, Chloe."

"Good boy," a female voice said, and Chloe dropped Ry's shoulder, whirling as best she could on her knees. Jack had also turned and had his gun out and pointed at the voice—but there was more than one woman standing around them. And they all had their own guns, trained at each of them.

Chloe stared at the trio in utter disbelief. It had been so long since she'd seen the woman with a gun pointed at Jack, she only recognized her because she saw so much of her own face in the woman.

Her mother.

The one with a gun trained on Chloe herself was also familiar. She'd had an off-again, on-again relationship with her father when Chloe was a teen. Sarah, if Chloe remembered correctly. It had been a volatile enough relationship that Chloe had once had to mop up the woman's bloody nose. She'd been fifteen at the time, maybe? The third woman, with a gun pointed square at Ry, looked vaguely familiar, but Chloe couldn't place her. Maybe another one of her father's girlfriend's? She was on the young side, so maybe one of Ry's?

Either way, Chloe didn't know what on earth to make of any of it. She looked at Jack. He had his sheriff's face on and was unreadable, gun held calmly and relaxed, pointed at Chloe's mother. But it was three guns to one.

"I'd put the gun down, Deputy," Jen Rogers said, smirking at Jack. "Or it's going to get real bloody, real quick."

"It's *Sheriff* these days, Jen." Because of course Jack had had dealings with her mother when he'd been a deputy for the county years ago. Why wouldn't he have?

"Well, *Sheriff*, put the gun down, or I start shooting."

Chapter Eighteen

Jack didn't immediately drop the weapon. If any of the women really wanted to shoot, they could have done it before drawing anyone's attention. They could have killed them all, then and there, because he and Chloe had been so intent on Ry.

A mistake. His own. But he couldn't worry about how he'd failed just yet. He had to get them out of this first.

"Sarah?" Jen—Chloe's mother—said, her gaze never leaving Jack's. "If he doesn't put the gun on the ground by the time I count to three, shoot her," she said, clearly referring to Chloe. "To kill."

Jack knew it wasn't a bluff. Part experience, part the look in Jen's eyes. He held his hands up in mock surrender, or maybe *temporary surrender* was a better term. Slowly, he crouched and gently laid the gun in front of him.

Just as slowly, he straightened.

"Courtney? Collect his gun."

The third gunman—someone Jack felt like he vaguely recognized, probably from run-ins with the law—scurried over and picked up his gun. Jack could have stopped her, but he was afraid it would prompt Jen or Sarah to start shooting.

Maybe they didn't want to take them all out, but he wouldn't put it past Jen.

Jen's attention turned from Jack to Chloe. "Didn't I always tell you to listen to your brother?"

"Yes, because you shared all his worst impulses," Chloe returned, her voice cool, calm and collected even as fury shone in her eyes.

But Jack was relieved she looked more mad than emotionally hurt, more determined than scared. They could get out of this if they kept their wits about them.

Or so he'd keep telling himself.

"Mom, make them let me go," Ry groused from where he sat on the ground, still handcuffed. "This hurts."

Jen looked at Ry sitting on the ground, eyes narrowed. "Do you think I'm *brainless*?"

Ry didn't meet his mother's gaze. He looked down at the ground. "No, ma'am."

"Get up, then. Your feet aren't cuffed, and your legs aren't broken. And stop whining."

Ry struggled to get up on his own. Jack didn't feel the need to help him, though Chloe was clearly fighting the impulse.

Jack considered the interaction between Ry and his mother. What Ry had said before Jen had shown up made him rethink…everything. Ry had clearly been working with these women, not with Mark Brink. But what did that mean for the murder? For the scrapbook that connected to the *Brink* family, not Jen Rogers? Why would she have hurt Hart, taken the scrapbook? Was it really all disparate parts that didn't connect? Or was there something bigger he couldn't fathom?

Jack wasn't sure which would be worse.

"Why'd you try to kidnap a cop, Mom?" Chloe asked, sounding bored.

"I didn't *try*. I succeeded," Jen snapped.

Jack wasn't sure it was smart to rile Jen up, considering she was clearly a violent criminal, but Chloe probably had a good sense of her own mother no matter how little they'd communicated recently. So he followed Chloe's lead.

"Why didn't you kill him, then?" he asked, keeping his voice and demeanor conversational. "Because we found him, and he'll survive. Probably ID you pretty quick, and then what?"

Jen barked out a laugh. "They'd have to *find* me. What do I care if they ID me? I could have killed him. Don't for a second think I couldn't have—or that I won't kill you." She waved the firearm in the air like she was swatting at an irritating gnat. "We didn't need a missing cop. That always makes your kind crawl out of your holes. Can't have one of your own disappearing, can you? Honestly, we would have left him bleeding in the parking lot, but we needed a little bit more time to create confusion."

She sighed heavily, surveying Jack and Chloe. "Cops. Always causing problems." She shook her head, then looked at the two women she was with. "We'll have to do this one special, girls."

The two women with her nodded like they knew what that meant. Jack did not think *special* was going to be good.

"What about him?" Courtney asked, gesturing her gun at Ry.

"Good question. Not sure yet. Let's get everyone home and go from there. Courtney, you take the lead. You three will follow. Sarah and I will handle the rear."

"Where are we going?" Chloe asked.

"On a fun little hike, sweetie. You just used to *love* those, didn't you? Anything to escape me, right?" Jen demanded, bitterness and something akin to hysteria tinging her tone.

Courtney started off down where Ry had initially run. There was no clear trail, but it was easy enough to follow the woman. Chloe walked stiffly at Jack's side, and Ry stumbled behind them. Unnecessarily, in Jack's estimation.

But Ry was in handcuffs. Chloe and he were free. They didn't have their weapons anymore, but they had training. Jack still had his pack on. Play their cards right, they could take down all three women without anyone getting too hurt, set off a flare, and end this here and now.

But the guns made it riskier than he liked. He'd have to bide his time.

Jack considered it his good fortune that he'd been over every last yard of the forest preserve, especially this area around the campground. Wherever the women took them, he'd have a general idea of where they were and where they'd need to go to get out.

He thought about the flare in his pack. The women hadn't searched it yet—clearly not quite the thorough criminals they fancied themselves. Not that he could currently use the flare, so maybe he shouldn't pat himself on the back just yet.

"Have they found him yet?" Jen asked. When the question was met with silence, she reached forward and tugged Chloe's ponytail. Hard.

Before he thought the move through, Jack reached forward and grabbed Jen's wrist to stop her from hurting Chloe. Which earned him a gun shoved into his chest.

He dropped Jen's wrist immediately, then held up his arms slowly. "Let's everyone keep their hands to themselves."

"Yeah, *let's*." She studied him through narrowed eyes, then Chloe.

"Have they found who?" Chloe asked, her voice devoid of any emotion. But when Jack slid a glance at her, her hands were curled into fists. Fury flickered in the depths of her dark eyes. And she was purposefully drawing her mother's attention away from *him*.

And it worked. "Your father, of course." Then Jen's mouth spread into a wide smile.

Jack was stunned silent. He hadn't known what to expect, but this was...

"You killed Dad?" Chloe said, sounding as shocked as he felt.

Jen laughed. "Of *course* I killed him. That's what this is about. That's what it's *always* been about."

There was something about the way she said *always* that settled in Jack all wrong. *Always.* Here in this campground. Where his parents had last been seen.

Always. Like *all* the way back. Like skeletal remains on a ranch Jen might not have owned but would have had access to at the time. Would have known where to bury bodies without them being found. "You killed my parents."

Jen flashed a grin at him. Mean and with a frantic kind of glee in her eyes. "You're finally catching on, *Sheriff.* Good for you."

CHLOE THOUGHT SHE was going to be sick. Of all the things she was prepared for, all the worst-case scenarios she'd considered, her mother's involvement in any of this had never once crossed her mind.

And it should have. Dad and Ry had always had a contentious relationship. Abusive, yes. Ry had been somewhat submissive to Dad on occasion. But they'd *fought*.

It was their mother who had true control over Ry. Always had. Chloe had just been under the impression Mom had taken off and was as no-contact with Ry as she was with Chloe.

Chloe tried to wrap her mind around it all. Years of… her mother being a cold-blooded killer from way back? Even if she couldn't put murder past her volatile mother, her killing Jack's parents just didn't make any sense that she could come up with.

So she asked the simplest, most concise question she couldn't swallow down. *"Why?"*

"You should learn a lesson, Chloe, from his bitch of a mother." She jerked her chin at Jack. "Sticking your nose where it doesn't belong is always going to come back to bite you in the ass."

She heard Jack's intake of breath, but she couldn't look at him just yet. She would crumble if she did. And if she reached out for him, comforted him in any way, her mother would see. And pounce on it like it was a weakness.

Chloe wouldn't be a weakness. She wouldn't risk Jack. Not now. They had to save each other. And she couldn't think about what this revelation meant to him if she was going to accomplish that.

"Move along now. Not much farther." Jen gestured with her gun, so Chloe felt she had no choice but to swallow and follow Courtney once more. Courtney led them through thick trees, over a tiny trickle of a creek and to the craggy rock face of a mountain.

Jen and Sarah came around to the front of them, stopping at a small crevice in the rock. Jen pointed at it. "In you go."

"Mom, you can't make me go in there with them!" Ry said, sounding like a petulant teenager. When he was a *grown* man. Would he ever get over himself? After this, if they survived, Chloe was finally going to have to accept the answer was no.

Jen stepped forward, up to Ry. Chloe recognized the expression on her face. It *looked* sympathetic, but that was how you knew something awful was coming.

Before Chloe could step in front of Ry—because old impulses die hard—their mother whipped her gun back and slammed it across Ry's face so he fell backward and onto his butt. Chloe tried to catch him, but she hadn't been fast enough.

"Get in the cave. Now," Jen said.

Chloe grabbed Ry by the elbow, and Jack grabbed his other. Pulling him toward the crevice, still cuffed. All while Ry moaned and sniveled.

Chloe hesitated at the opening of the crevice. All dark. All black. A small, little opening. Chloe wasn't even sure Jack would be able to fit through if he tried. She tried to swallow an old panic fluttering around in her stomach. She didn't like heights and she didn't like enclosed spaces.

She had learned to keep her fear of heights hidden from her parents, but only because her fear of enclosed spaces had been something she hadn't known she should hide until her parents had used it against her when she was a little girl. Mom especially. She'd loved to lock her in the little closet in their apartment in town.

Chloe had to focus very hard on not remembering, on not going back to those old feelings of being a helpless little girl. She was an adult. She was a cop. She could handle this. She could survive it—just like she had then.

"Go on, Chloe. Get in there," Mom said in a little sing-songy voice, clearly reading her panic and enjoying it.

Chloe took a deep, steadying breath. She wouldn't give her mother the satisfaction of panic. Not when she had to somehow protect Ry and Jack from whatever this turned out to be.

Because if she'd confessed to essentially three murders, Jen had no plans to let them go. Maybe she wasn't ready to kill them yet for some unknown reason, but that had to be the plan.

"I'll go first," Jack murmured as they approached the rock. "Push Ry in after me, and I'll pull. Then you." He looked at her, right in the eye. "Got it?"

He was trying to be her anchor, and she appreciated it. Because she needed one, and if anyone could be one, it was him. Jack Hudson.

Who is in this mess because of you. Whose parents are gone because of yours.

And who loved her anyway, she reminded herself. Because he did. She saw it in his eyes, in his move to protect her *and* Ry. So she would be strong for him as much as for herself.

Jack flattened himself against one side of the rock and shuffled in through the crevice, just barely making it. Chloe couldn't see him, but she pictured his dark, steady gaze and helped Ry maneuver himself inside as well.

She glanced back at the trio of women with guns. She knew she shouldn't do it, shouldn't give her mother a chance to see her fear. But it was her mother she studied now.

"What are you doing, Mom?"

Mom's mouth curved into a vicious smile. "Ruining as many lives as I can. Just like how your father and high-and-mighty Laura Hudson tried to ruin mine."

It made no sense. It had never made any sense. Her mother's unending well of anger, of blame, of needing to hurt anyone and everyone she could reach.

"Get inside, Chloe. Or I start shooting."

Chloe nodded and then pushed herself through the crevice. Inside, it was so dark. Damp and cold and dark and—

A hand clasped around her forearm and gently pulled her inside.

Jack.

She wanted to lean into him, but she was afraid to allow herself the weakness. Afraid of what her mother might see and use against her.

So she held herself upright and tried to allow her eyes to adjust to the dark. But not long after they'd all gotten inside, a light clicked on. A lantern, some battery-powered thing hanging from a hook dug into the rock face. The cave was much bigger than the crevice had let on and was full of things. Makeshift beds, a table, a whole little outdoor-kitchen setup. Like people lived here.

Mom had said *home*. Was this… Was *this* where she'd been living all these years? It didn't make any sense, except that it explained why no one had been able to find her. A cave in a remote forest preserve.

But…why?

Chloe watched as Sarah settled herself in a chair at the entrance of the cave, gun pointed in their direction. Had the three of them been together all this time? She understood them conspiring to kill her father. And they'd clearly spent years planning it, as Mark had been in prison for six years now.

But Jack's parents… So many years ago. It just made no sense.

"Make yourselves comfortable," Sarah said with a mean smile.

Mom entered, standing next to Sarah, scowling. "For the love of God, shut him up," she said, referring to Ry.

Chloe looked down at her brother. His mouth was bleeding, and he was making little whimpering noises. Chloe felt a mix of worry and sympathy and bone-deep anger that he'd been part of this at all. "Come on, Ry, buck up," she told him. Just like she had when they were kids and she had to be the strong one. The one to protect them both.

He glared up at her, anger in his gaze. Anger when he was half the reason they were here. For so many years, she'd given him a pass. Because their childhood had been rough. She'd blamed herself for not being strong enough, smart enough, *good* enough to save him from all the trouble *he* caused.

But she'd had no one, and she'd turned out okay. Better than okay. She'd cobbled together a damn good life for herself, and Ry had complained and blamed and worn his victimhood like a second skin.

Chloe just wished she'd realized all this sooner.

"I thought you didn't want the hassle of cops trying to find other cops," Jack said, sounding so calm and in control. He couldn't be, though. Not knowing the woman standing in front of him had killed his parents. He was holding on to their training. He was dealing with the crisis at hand.

Chloe felt like everything she'd ever learned about being a cop, about de-escalating a situation, about self-preservation, had deserted her. Her entire world twisted inside out.

Except Jack.

Jen smirked at him. "Sure, it's a hassle when you don't have time to do it right. When there's too many witnesses. Now I have all the time in the world to make sure you all end up just like your parents, Sheriff. Because that's what happens to people who butt their noses in where they don't belong. They *disappear* without a trace."

Chapter Nineteen

Without a trace. Those words landed like blows because it was true. His parents had disappeared without a trace. Jen had committed a crime that she'd escaped for seventeen years, and Jack still wasn't sure what had prompted Ry to find those remains—accident, on purpose, it didn't matter.

Jen Rogers knew how to get away with murder, and he had to put that knowledge away. Set it aside so they could figure out how not to be her next victims.

Jack wondered if Jen knew they had a group of people already on-site. People who, come four o'clock, would start looking for them. And knew exactly where they'd been. Had she been watching them all this time, or had she stumbled upon them in the campground simply because of Ry?

He considered bringing it up to see if it would prompt Jen to panic, to make a mistake. That's all he needed. One little mistake.

"Now, I want both your cell phones," Jen said, holding out her free hand.

"What are you going to do with those? We don't have service in a cave. Can't ping us in here."

"It's called *distraction*, Sheriff. Now, hand them over."

Jack reached into his pocket. He considered "accidentally" dropping the phone. Destroying it rather than have it be used

against him. But Chloe was taking hers out. She looked back
at him and held her hand out like she'd take his too. So he
tried to give it to her.

But she didn't take it. She put hers in *his* hand and gave
him a look. A meaningful look.

Then he realized what she was trying to tell him. She
had that damn smartwatch on her wrist. No one would be
able to track them in this *cave*, but it was something. A potential lifeline. Without reacting, he took the two phones
and walked them over to Jen. He handed them out to her.

She took them. Then she smiled at him. "You look like
your dad."

Even knowing it was meant to hurt, meant to elicit a reaction, he couldn't stop it from landing. He *did* look like a
carbon copy of Dean Hudson. He was reminded every time
he looked in the mirror of the father he lost all too soon.

"Your mother could have survived, you know."

Jack held Jen's mean gaze. Inside, he was a riot of pain,
but he kept his expression bland. And he said nothing.

"It could have just been your worthless father. Trying
to tell me how to parent my children. Trying to get me into
trouble with all those nosy family-service agents." Jen's
self-satisfied smirk faded into an angry scowl, like she
was reliving it. "I would have settled for just taking him
out. She could have escaped. But she had to try and save
your father."

"It's what people with souls do, Jen," Jack returned, ignoring how rough his voice sounded. "Help each other.
Save each other. Love each other."

"No one's ever done that for me!" she shouted, stomping
her foot like a child. And Jack could see where Ry had got-

ten some of his self-victimization. It stemmed from right
here. He could almost feel bad for the guy. Almost.

Jen kept on shrieking. "No one did anything for me,
ever!"

Jack shrugged. "Sounds like you deserved it."

Even in the orangish glow of the lantern light, he could
see her face mottled red with rage. Her hands had curled
into fists. Sarah murmured something softly to her, and
Jen inhaled sharply, then let it out slowly. Calming herself, minute by minute, until she aimed one of her nasty
smiles at him again.

"I want you to know, they died begging for mercy."

He should let it go—God knew, he should let it go. But
when it came to his parents, their memory, he couldn't
let her have the last word. "Sounds like they died fighting for it."

She let out a cry of rage then, guttural and furious. She
wrenched back her arm. Jack went with instinct and blocked
the blow by grabbing her arm before she could slam the
gun across his face like she'd done to Ry.

It was a mistake—he knew that the minute his hand had
come into contact with her arm. But it was just instinct,
self-preservation.

It was pure stubbornness and anger that kept his grip on
her arm. Until she lifted her left hand, and there was a gun
in that one too. Pointed right at his head. *Then* he thought
better of his fury and hurt.

"No!" It was, shockingly, Sarah's voice. She leaped off
the chair, grabbed Jen's left arm. Jack still hadn't let go of
her right. So she was now being held—on one side by her
partner and on one side by her victim.

"You can't shoot him," Sarah said, seeming afraid. Des-

perate. "It's not the plan. You said it yourself. We can't devi-
ate from the plan. We've already messed up once. We can't
mess up again. It all goes to hell. You *know* that."

Jack was so surprised by the unexpected save that when
Jen ripped her arm out of his grasp, he didn't even try to
hold on. He stepped back, giving the women the space for
their argument, and hopefully the distraction was enough so
that Jen's anger was pointed to the woman she worked with.

Maybe that was a weakness that would allow them to
escape.

"They're *my* plans," Jen said, her entire body turning
toward Sarah. Her back to Jack and Chloe and Ry behind
them. Like none of them even mattered. Like they couldn't
be a threat.

Could he tackle her now, Jack considered? Would Chloe
be able to get to Sarah's gun in time to take her out before
retaliation? But that still left Courtney, who was presumably outside the cave.

But what if she wasn't? Was it worth the risk? Jack
kept himself ready, watching, waiting for just the right
moment—and he knew Chloe beside him was doing the
same exact thing. Poised and ready to lunge.

He wanted it to be now, but it wasn't. But they would
know when it was. They'd be ready. He believed that.

He had to.

"Any mistakes today have been *your* fault. I think you
know that," Jen was yelling at Sarah.

Sarah's eyes widened, a mix of fear and offense. Panic,
maybe. But she stood up to Jen. "I do *not* know that! It
was your plan that was faulty. We did everything you said!
Courtney got Ry to lure Mark here. *I* took the first shot and
didn't kill him. *Just* like you said. I—"

"You hesitated! You know you hesitated! If you'd taken that shot when you were supposed to, I could trust you. But now? I can't. So I think we need to retool our plan."

Sarah was shaking her head. "We have to stick to the plan, or we'll get caught! I'm not getting caught!" She pointed her finger in Jen's face, panic mounting. "I'll tell the cops *everything*. I'll tell them it was your idea, your plan. Lure Mark here. Get Chloe away from the scrapbook. I'll tell them—"

The sound of a bullet exploding out of a gun erupted around them. Instinct had Jack jumping back toward Chloe, who'd hit the deck with her hands over her ears.

When he looked up, he saw Jen holding a gun in each hand while Sarah lay on the ground, still and lifeless. A pool of blood slowly growing bigger around her.

"You won't be able to tell them anything now, will you?" Jen said to Sarah's lifeless form. She blew out a breath, shrugged her shoulders a few times like she was shrugging away tension. "Man, I feel better." She turned to face them, evil smile back in place. "Now. It's time for a new plan."

THE GUNSHOT WAS still echoing in Chloe's ears. She didn't let herself look at the dead woman on the ground. She looked up from the defensive position she'd fallen into and focused on the woman who might kill them all.

Chloe couldn't remember ever loving her mother. Even when she was a little girl, too young to understand her childhood was a dangerous disaster, she'd wondered why her mother had bothered to have one child, let alone two.

And still, this was all such a shock. Bits and pieces she could make sense of, but the whole of what was happening, what had happened, was just too bizarre to fully fathom.

Clearly Mom's plan had been to kill Mark and get away with it. She was teaming up with Mark's other victims to do it. She'd killed Jack's parents because they'd called family services on her.

But what did it have to do with the scrapbook?

There were no answers to that yet. No answers could come if they didn't survive.

So she focused on the one most important thing to her.

She would find a way to get Jack out of this. She certainly wasn't about to let her mother make another Hudson a victim of her sociopathic ways. No matter what. Chloe would do anything and everything to get him out.

"Now you have more bodies to clean up," Chloe pointed out. Her voice was steady, her tone cool. She kept her expression blank when her mother turned to sneer at her.

"It's not about the bodies. That's easy." She gestured at the cave. Like…there were bodies back there, deeper in the cavern. A shudder chased down Chloe's spine, though she ignored it.

"And some bodies, like your father's, don't matter. No one will care that Mark Brink was murdered in cold blood. They'll do some cursory due diligence, then mark it down to his past." Her lips curled back even farther. "*Hudsons* and *cops* are different, though. We've got to make sure there's no trace. It's not about *bodies*, it's about trails."

"Forensic investigations have come a long way in seventeen years. You'd be surprised how easy it is to pin you to Mark Brink's murder," Jack said blandly.

Every time she poked at her mother, he did too. He took her lead and ran with it. It gave her hope that somehow they could outsmart her mother. They were good cops, a good team. They could do it. They just needed a chance.

Jen took a threatening step toward Jack, those guns in her hands making Chloe have to fight the need to step between Jack and her mother. To protect him.

It would be a death sentence for him. Chloe knew that.

"Even if they could pin it on me, even if they bothered, they couldn't find me. Do you know how long I've been here? Right here. Living, loving and laughing my ass off while no one could find *anything* about your do-gooder parents."

The whole time. Ever since Mom had just not come home one day and Chloe had spent the next few years struggling to keep Ry on the straight and narrow, trying to keep Dad from ruining their lives. Mom hadn't been running away, chasing a score or a guy or whatever.

She'd been living in a *cave*? "But why hide if no one knew you'd murdered the Hudsons?"

"Your *father* was meant to stumble over those remains and get himself into a heap of trouble. Your *father* was supposed to take the fall. But he never did listen, did he? He never followed through or did what he should. So I had to adjust my plans. You see, Chloe, one thing you never could understand was the beauty of *patience*. Always had to be going, moving, doing. Sometimes sitting and waiting is the best thing in the world. Because no one will ever know. And Mark Brink is dead. Finally."

Chloe didn't see how sitting and waiting had been best for her mother. Jen had always been mean, cruel, narcissistic and rotten to the core. But she had never been quite this unhinged, or so it had seemed to Chloe at the time. Chloe supposed she should be grateful because *unhinged* left room for error. One little mistake and Chloe or Jack would take advantage of it and get out of this.

Chloe was sure of it.

Courtney stepped through the cave entrance. She nearly stumbled when she saw the body on the floor, but aside from a wide-eyed expression, she didn't voice any surprise. She blinked once, then turned toward Jen.

"A couple saw them running after Ry and called the police." Her voice betrayed her a little. It shook.

"Damn interfering busybodies," Jen said grimly. "They'll be crawling all over now."

"I don't think we should do it here," Courtney said, eyeing Chloe, Jack and Ry before turning her attention back to Jen. "We need to move."

Chloe didn't know what *do it here* meant for sure, but she had a bad feeling it meant *kill them*.

Jen shook her head. "Moving is too dangerous with cops crawling around. We need a distraction. Time and a distraction." She turned to face them. "Ry, get over here."

Chloe looked over her shoulder and watched as her brother struggled to his feet, keeping his eyes downcast and refusing to meet her gaze as he shuffled over to their mother.

"You're going to go out to that campground. You're going to let a cop find you—don't you go searching them out, just let them find you. You're going to hedge, lie a little bit, take your time, but eventually you'll confess you saw your sister and the sheriff, and you told them where the scrapbook is."

"They'll arrest me if they think I had anything to do with the scrapbook!"

Jen laughed. Low and mean. "Yeah, so what? A lot worse happens if you don't." She jerked her gaze to Jack. "Uncuff him. And give him that backpack you've got on. That'll prove he saw you guys."

Jack didn't respond right away. He looked at Chloe. She couldn't think of a way to get out of this—and as much as it pained her to be thinking about Ry's well-being after all this, Ry would be safer in jail than he was here. So she gave Jack a little nod.

He pulled the key out of his pocket and tossed it toward Jen. She didn't catch it, but she did scowl at him. "I can't *wait* to make your death slow and painful."

"I've never known a drawn-out murder to work out for the murderer," Jack replied.

Jen's smile was pure *evil*. "Remind me to give you a step-by-step of how I took my sweet time with your parents." She picked up the key he'd thrown. "But first things first." Roughly, she jammed the key into the cuffs and released Ry.

"You tell them you sent them off to find the scrapbook. You tell them Mark told you he left it in a hotel room in Hardy. You don't know the specifics, but that's what he told you, so that's what you told them. Do you understand?"

Ry nodded.

"If you don't do exactly as I say, what happens?"

"The pit," he said, sounding like the little boy Chloe remembered all too well. Not always sweet, but always trusting.

Chloe didn't know what *the pit* was—no doubt some kind of torture. Mom was always good at that.

"You didn't like your last stint in the pit, did you?"

Ry shook his head vehemently.

"What's better, Rylan? The pit or getting arrested?"

"Arrested," Ry muttered.

"That's right. Go get the backpack off him," she said, pointing to Jack.

Ry trudged over. He didn't meet Chloe's gaze or Jack's,

just kept his eyes on the ground and held out his hand. When Jack didn't immediately hand it over, Ry slowly looked up.

Even slower, Jack shrugged the backpack off. With careful, precise movements, he held it out to Ry. When he spoke, it was low and quiet. Maybe Jen heard over by the entrance, maybe she didn't, but Chloe figured it didn't matter. It was only the truth.

"She deserved better, Ry."

Ry didn't say anything, didn't even give her a glance. He just took the bag and scurried back over to their mother.

"Not one wrong move, Rylan. Not *one*," Jen said menacingly.

He gave a little nod. He took a step toward the cave entrance but then looked back at her and Jack. "Sorry, Chlo," he said, before Jen pushed him out the crevice of the entrance.

It was funny. She almost believed he was.

But what she didn't believe was that he'd help.

Chapter Twenty

Jack knew better than to count on Ry going against his mother's wishes and helping them out of this mess, but he hoped for Chloe's sake Ry might mess up his assignment somehow. If he ran into Zeke or Carlyle back at that campground, they'd surely see through him. They'd retrace his steps.

Or, if he had even an ounce of intelligence, he'd use the flare in the pack and really help them.

But Jack wouldn't depend on Ry to fix this for them. He and Chloe would have to devise a plan. One that took into account that his family was out there and would start looking for them. All they had to do was stay alive past four o'clock.

"Do you think he's actually going to listen?" Courtney asked Jen in a low voice, but in the cave, it carried over to him and Chloe.

"He knows what happens to him if he doesn't," Jen replied darkly.

"What if—"

"That boy is a *coward*. Always has been. Always will be. Besides, we have secret weapons. So *many* secrets. Let's go show them one." She turned her attention from Courtney to Jack and Chloe. "You're going to turn around. You're going to start walking. And you're not going to stop until I tell you to."

Jack shared a look with Chloe. It was two against two now, and going deeper in the cave was only asking for trouble when it was clear Jen's plan was to kill them. Why keep giving her easier and easier ways to get away with it?

"I don't think we will, Jen."

Chloe inhaled sharply, but she nodded. She moved so that they stood shoulder to shoulder, facing Jen and Courtney and eyeing the cave exit behind them. All they had to do was get past them without getting shot.

Without getting *fatally* shot, really. He knew Chloe wouldn't appreciate it, but if *he* drew both their gunfire, she could get past them. Get out. Maybe there'd be a chance. Oh, she wouldn't thank him for that. She'd end up beating herself up for it, especially if he did get fatally wounded.

But she'd be alive.

"You will because if you recall, *I've* got the upper hand. *All* of the upper hands. You do what I say."

"So we can die the way you want us to?" Chloe shook her head. "Pass."

"Pass?" Jen replied, then she laughed. High-pitched and out of control. "*Pass*, she says. Oh, Chloe, you did not inherit *any* of the Rogers family smarts, did you?"

"I hope to God not."

Jen was aiming her gun at Chloe now, and Jack knew he needed to do something. Intervene before she ended up dead here in this dark damn cave. Not on his watch.

"It seems to me this only works out for you if we follow what you say. I don't think we have much interest in this working out for you, so I guess we're at an impasse. I guess you'll have to shoot us." He tried to angle his body so he was in front of Chloe, but she was doing the same thing to him.

He wanted to tell her to quit it, wanted to shove her out of the way, which distracted him enough that he wasn't giving Jen the attention he should have been.

"As you wish," Jen replied with a shrug. Then he didn't have a chance to so much as blink. Jen must have pulled the trigger as she lifted the gun. The pain that blasted through his shoulder was more shock than the sound of the gun going off.

CHLOE FORGOT EVERYTHING in that moment. Every minute of training, every potential threat around them. She only saw Jack stumble back and blood bloom on his shoulder, and she leaped for him.

She looked around wildly for something to stop the bleeding and came up with nothing. *Nothing.*

"I'm okay. It's okay," he said, but he did not sound like himself. He was in pain. He had been *shot*.

"It's not okay," she returned, pulling the hem of her shirt into as much of a ball as she could and pressing it to his shoulder.

His hissed out a pained breath. "Trying to convince myself here, Chloe." He swore once, twice. He didn't sit still, moving around as if trying to find some comfortable position, even though a *bullet* had passed through his shoulder.

"Stop moving. I have to put pressure on it. I have to—" The yank at her hair took her by surprise because she'd let panic and worry and *love* blind her to the imminent threat. She fell back as Jen stepped forward.

"Am I clear now? You can either fight and die right here or you can get on your feet and move."

Chloe held Jack's pained gaze. She couldn't let him die here. She couldn't. But they couldn't go deeper into this cave. Not with his wound, not with her mother's plans clear. Jen wanted it too much, when it would be so easy to just shoot them right now.

Clearly she had something deeper in the cave where she thought she could kill them and get away with it. Chloe would die before she gave her mother that.

It had to end right now. "Sounds like it's easier for you if we move. So maybe we choose to die right here."

"Do you think I won't shoot you both?"

Chloe knew she would. Knew this wasn't looking good. But if they walked any farther, it would be over. And maybe no one would ever find them. Another Hudson mystery.

No. She wouldn't let that happen. "If you're going to kill us, I'd much prefer you get caught."

Fury stamped all over her mother's features. It reminded Chloe too much of a childhood she'd spent a lot of time blocking out. Her therapist had told her not remembering a lot was a *bad sign*, and now Chloe fully understood what she meant by that. She'd blocked out *this*. That violence. That total lack of empathy for another human being.

Chloe didn't want to leave Jack's side, but she forced herself to stand. To face her mother. "And if you're going to kill us anyway, I might as well *fight*." She took a few steps forward, bracing herself for pain, for a gunshot wound to stop her in her tracks.

But instead, there was a voice.

"Drop your weapons."

Chloe whirled around, and nearly wept right then. Carlyle stood next to her brother, Zeke, both with guns trained on Jen and Courtney.

But Chloe also knew her mother. So she dove immediately into her mother's legs, hoping to knock her off her feet so she wouldn't have a chance to shoot *anyone*. It worked. Jen tumbled down on top of Chloe, but not before another gunshot went off.

Hopefully Carlyle's or Zeke's. *Please, God.* She scrambled out from her mother's weight. Jen kicked, clawed, pulled, but Chloe could fight too. She managed to get the gun from her mother, to wrestle her into submission.

Zeke came over to her and knelt on the other side of Jen, pulling out a zip-tie and using it to bind her hands together. Chloe looked over at Courtney. She was in the same position as Jen now, so Zeke must have gotten her first.

Chloe pushed to her feet. They needed to get Jack to the hospital. A gunshot wound to his shoulder wasn't good, but if they could get him…

He was lying completely prone on the floor now. More blood. Not just on his shoulder, but lower. Carlyle had something pressed to his abdomen. He'd been shot again. *No, no, no.*

She scrambled over to him. Repeating his name. Maybe crying. She didn't know. But he was pale, and he wasn't moving or responding to her in any way and *oh God*.

"He's breathing, Chloe," Carlyle said sharply. "So put something on that shoulder."

Chloe looked around for something, even as tears clouded her vision. But then chaos erupted around them. Just absolute chaos. Screaming. Yelling. Pounding footsteps. But she just concentrated on Jack's breathing. Because he was breathing. She felt like as long as she stayed here, her hand on his chest, his heart, she could *will* him to keep breathing. As long as he was breathing…

Someone pulled her off, and she fought them. If they pulled her away… If…

"Let the medics help," Zeke said, firm and authoritative in her ear as he banded her arms at her sides to stop her from fighting him.

Carlyle stepped in front of her, blocking her view of Jack. Jack. Who'd been shot twice. *Twice*. Because of her.

"They're going to take him to the hospital. He's going to be okay," Carlyle said.

"How do you know?" Chloe demanded.

And Carlyle didn't answer. Because the truth was, he might not be. And she would always have to live with that.

Zeke's grip on her loosened. She would have crumpled then and there, but Carlyle held her up by an arm. Medics were working to find a way to get Jack out of the small crevice of the entrance.

A couple of cops had Jen and Courtney cuffed, face down on the cave ground. They screamed and argued and fought, but they weren't going to be a problem anymore. They were going to go to prison. For murder. Multiple murders.

It should have been a relief, but nothing would feel like relief until she knew Jack would be okay.

They had to stand in this awful cave while the medics got Jack out, while the police got Jen and Courtney out. Chloe would have hyperventilated if not for Carlyle rubbing a supportive hand up and down her back.

When they were finally given the go-ahead to leave, Chloe knew there'd be questions. So many questions. But she wouldn't be able to answer any of them until Jack was okay.

When she emerged from the cave, she saw her brother.

He was cuffed, sitting on the ground, a deputy talking down at him.

She could only stare. He'd betrayed her. He was part of *all* this. When he looked up and saw her glaring at him, his eyes got big and shiny.

"I know I messed up, Chlo, but I fixed it. Didn't I?" he called across the distance between them. Cops looked at her; Hudsons looked at her.

She stared at her brother.

"He found Zeke and I," Carlyle said quietly, standing next to her. But Chloe could hear the disgust in Carlyle's voice. "We were pretty close, but we hadn't found the entrance to the cave. He is why we found you in the nick of time, and we didn't have to shake it out of him."

She wanted to feel good. She wanted to feel relief. Her brother wasn't all bad. He'd helped. Even with Mom threatening him the way she had, he had asked Carlyle and Zeke for help. He'd done the right thing.

She wanted to believe that, but she saw him sitting there and knew he'd just done the *easiest* thing. Because he always did. So she just felt *angry*. Because Jack was hurt. And sometimes doing the right thing was too little, too late.

She walked over to him. He wanted reassurance. He wanted to know he'd done okay. After being such a huge part of how this had all gone so badly. Years ago, she would have reassured him. Forgiven him.

Today, she had nothing left. "If he dies, I'll never, ever speak to you again," she said. "I will never lay eyes on you again. I will never, ever have anything to do with you. Ever."

Ry's eyes widened, and the hope in them died. "You're choosing him over me?"

"No, Ry. I'm choosing *me* over you. I will always love

you, but I can't be part of your life anymore. Not until you can take some responsibility for it. Maybe jail will teach you that. Maybe it won't. I won't know because I won't be in contact. I won't be helping. I'm done." She should have said all those things years ago. Now, just like him, it was too little, too late.

But she'd done it.

"That isn't fair!" he yelled. After all he'd done, he thought anything should be *fair*.

She shook her head and walked away from her brother. She hoped someday he'd find some better version of himself. But until he did…she was done.

Chapter Twenty-One

Jack thought he heard a baby crying. Where had a baby come from? It was nighttime. Somewhere. Where was he?

Cave. Cave? The cave and— *Chloe*. He tried to say her name, but nothing came out of his mouth except a raspy kind of noise. He couldn't seem to open his eyes. Heavy, too heavy. After the spurt of panic, he told himself to breathe, to count, to settle. He couldn't protect anyone if he couldn't open his eyes.

He started to become aware of things. The beep of machines, the feel of something on his arm. The sound of people shuffling. He managed to open his eyes to bright, blinding white. Hospital.

Well, he was here, so he had to be alive, he supposed. But then he caught sight of a woman. A woman with dark hair and soft eyes. Maybe he was dead after all. "Mom?"

But it only took a second or two to realize it wasn't his mother. It was Mary. "Sorry," he rasped.

Her smile was a little strange, definitely teary. He tried to get his brain to engage as he looked at her standing there next to his hospital bed. She looked different. She had a little bundle in her arms. Even with his brain fuzzy, that all made sense to him. "Mary."

"Sorry Walker couldn't help you guys. We were a little busy."

"You had the baby." A baby. He'd been fighting for his life, and she'd been giving birth. What a strange, strange life.

Both his sisters had *babies*. He remembered *them* being babies, and now they were mothers. His brain was too fuzzy to fully comprehend all this. He wanted to sit up. He wanted to ask a million questions.

"You're going to have to hurry up and get better so you can hold him," she said. She didn't cry, but he could hear the pain and fear in her voice.

"I'm okay." Of course, he had no idea if that was true. He'd been shot. Twice, if he remembered correctly. He tried to move, but he couldn't quite manage and the pain was starting to flutter above the fuzzy feeling.

"You will be. We'll all baby you till you are."

"I can't sit up. Let me see him, huh?"

She tilted the bundle until he could see the scrunched up little face of a sleeping newborn with a shock of dark hair.

"The problem is, I married a man whose last name is Daniels."

Jack didn't quite follow. "Why is that a problem?"

"I could hardly name my son Jack Daniels," Mary replied, looking lovingly down at the newborn in her arms.

"Why would…" He wanted to shift uncomfortably. "You don't have to name anyone after me."

Her eyes were full of tears. "Of course I don't have to. But I wanted to—Walker and I wanted to name our son after the best men we knew. You're at the top of that list, for both of us. I want that legacy for my son. I wanted him to have someone he knew, someone he'd spend his life looking up to. So he always knew what was right. Because his namesake would be right there, showing him."

Jack was completely and utterly speechless. "Well." But he remembered Chloe talking about legacies, and ghosts and how being sad is not all that bad. It felt like a million years ago.

"So, we did the best we could, all things considered," Mary said with a little sniff. She used her shoulder to wipe a tear off her cheek. "This is Jackson Dean Daniels. If we end up shortening it, he can go by JD. But it's after you, it's because of you. His name. Who we all are." She started crying again, tears rolling down her cheeks. "I'm so glad you're okay."

Okay. That cave. Today. This whole thing. "Chloe? Ry? I... I don't remember exactly..." Chloe had been okay. She had been. Had to be.

"They're both fine. Carlyle and Zeke got to you guys just in time. Jen Rogers and her two accomplices have been charged with the murder of Mark Brink and our parents. I knew you'd want the details, and they're still wading through them all. But everything with the bones, with the snake and Detective Hart, it was all part of planning to murder Mark without Chloe getting any wind of it."

Jack closed his eyes. His mind was whirling in too many directions. He wanted to see Chloe. Wanted to see for himself she was okay, but she wasn't here. Mary was and...

And after sixteen years, they finally knew. "We've got answers now, Mary. Who killed Mom and Dad. Why... If you can call it a why. Everything we tried to find all these years."

"It's so strange," she said, her voice a creaky whisper. "I just don't care."

He managed to open his eyes, and she was gazing down at her son, those tears still on her cheeks. She kept talking. "You're okay, and I have him. We all have…so much. It's a tragedy to have lost them. It'll always be a tragedy. But answers didn't change anything. Us all living our lives on the foundations they gave us. That's the only thing that matters."

It was such a strange thing, to agree. After years of thinking having answers would change something in his life, he now had those answers and nothing changed. Not really.

"Mary, where's Chloe?"

"She's fine."

"That isn't what I asked."

"She… We aren't sure where she went. She got checked out by doctors, answered all the police's questions, but we kind of lost her in the fray. It's okay. Carlyle and Anna are out trying to track her down, but we know she's okay."

He tried to sit up, but he couldn't. He cursed his own weaknesses. Cursed everything. "She's going to blame herself. She can't seem to help it. I just—"

"Don't worry, Jack. We'll find her, and we're all going to make sure she knows just where she belongs."

Here. She belonged right *here.*

CHLOE KNEW SHE couldn't just sit in the hospital parking lot forever. She had to act. She had to… She didn't want to see him, and she didn't think she'd ever be able to breathe again if she didn't see with her own two eyes that he was okay.

He wouldn't blame her. He'd be irritated she blamed herself. She understood all these things rationally, but she could not seem to move past all the swirling things she knew about Jack and who he was and the horrible things she felt about herself.

Hey, this is why we go to therapy. Well, she'd have a doozy of a session at her next appointment.

"What the hell are you doing here?"

Chloe looked up to see Carlyle stalking up to her, Anna not far behind.

"We've been looking all over for you," Anna said.

Chloe shook her head. "You should be with Jack. You should—"

"And who do you think Jack wants to see?" Anna returned. "Come on. Get up. Let's go."

They stood on either side of her, taking her by the arms and hauling her to her feet. But she didn't let them pull her to the door.

"I can't go in. I wanted to. I just…"

They didn't let her go, but they did stop trying to pull her.

"Chloe, you've had a day," Anna said, as gently as Chloe had ever heard her say anything. "But neither you nor Jack are going to rest until you see each other. Trust me. I know." Because her husband had been shot last year, and she'd been hurt too. So maybe she was right, but…

"My mother killed your parents, Anna."

"Yeah. Hell of a thing."

Like it was that simple. "My brother made it worse. Everything…it all connects to *me*."

"Self-centered much?" Carlyle said under her breath, making Anna snort out a laugh.

"I just want to curl up and die." Which was not something she would have ever admitted to out loud if she wasn't having a *day*, she supposed. And she didn't really want to die. She just wanted…

"Wow, that's super melodramatic," Carlyle said, and she was gently tugging her forward.

"I'm impressed. I didn't think you had it in you," Anna added, also applying pressure to move her forward.

"You guys…"

"Chloe, we know you. All of us. I get it, better than most, how having a parent with that kind of evil in them can mess you up, but you're too well loved to let what other people have chosen ruin your life."

Too well loved. Ouch.

"*And* Jack loves you. He needs to see you. And since you love him, you're going to get over yourself and go see him." Anna gave her yet another tug.

Chloe didn't know how to argue with that, so she was somehow being pulled down hospital corridors and to a hospital-room door. Anna shoved it open. "Go on, now." Then Anna and Carlyle stood shoulder to shoulder like they were blocking any potential exit.

So Chloe *had* to step in. Had to look.

Jack was in a hospital bed. Hooked up to all sorts of awful things. But his eyes were open, and he was talking to Mary.

Chloe must have made a noise, because Mary turned, and Jack looked over at her. She would have kept looking at Jack, but Mary was holding something. She was… "Mary… You… You had the baby."

In the middle of all this *awful*, a baby had been born.

Mary smiled at her and took a few steps closer, holding the baby so Chloe could see his face. "Meet Jackson Dean Daniels."

Chloe looked at the little newborn. She'd never been

around babies much. The little bundle seemed like an alien lifeform to her. And still…

"He's perfect." She couldn't help but smile down at the baby, especially when he blinked open his deep blue eyes and seemed to be squinting at her in suspicion. "Perfect." *Jackson.* After Jack, no doubt.

It made her want to cry all over again.

"I think so," Mary agreed. Then she looked at the doorway. Chloe looked over her shoulder to see Walker standing there.

"Good to see you both in one piece," he offered, presumably to Chloe and Jack. But he didn't tear his gaze away from Mary or the bundle in her arms. "Time's up, honey. You need to rest."

Mary nodded, but as she passed Chloe, she leaned close. "Stay with him until someone else comes, okay? I don't want him alone."

Chloe wanted to argue. She wanted to run away. But that was just childish and probably her exhaustion talking. She nodded at Mary, then hesitantly moved closer to Jack in the bed.

He looked too big for it. Too vital. He'd been shot twice. Gone through surgery. And still he seemed just like himself. When she felt like a bag of broken, rusty, disparate parts.

"Hi," she offered.

"Hi," he returned. And said nothing else. Just kept that steady gaze on hers.

Everything inside her felt bruised. He didn't say anything, just looked at her with dark eyes. But she had seen that expression on his face for a while now. In every smile, in every secret goodbye in the dark, in the way he protected her. In the way he let her in when he let no one else in.

And still, all the ways today connected to her felt like a wall she couldn't cross. So she fell back on what she usually used as a shield. That cop persona she'd developed.

"The police arrested everyone, including Ry. They're all turning on each other, so sentencing should be straightforward once they get that far. There are still some questions. The scrapbook is missing, and no one will spill on why it's so important. So there's work to be done. Bent County will handle it, though."

He gave a little nod but still didn't speak.

"Jack, I—"

"I need you to do me a favor," he said, cutting her off, even though his voice was weak and raspy.

And because it was, she immediately swallowed the apology. She'd do anything for him. Always. "Okay."

"I need you to never, ever, for the rest of our lives, say you're sorry to me about this."

She should have known. "Jack—"

"Listen to me. It hurts. It hurts to watch you blame yourself when you dug your way out of all that trauma, all that awful, and made yourself into a smart, *honorable*, wonderful person. I don't look at you and see them. Never did. Never will. And I know you can't magically wipe away any feelings you have on the matter. I get that they're complicated and messy, but I love you no matter what. So I can't take any apologies when *you* have nothing to apologize for. Okay?"

She *knew* he was right, but she hadn't felt it. Until he said it. Then it was like... God, she could breathe again, even as tears filled her eyes. She took the rest of the steps so she stood next to the bed now. She wiped at her eyes with the backs of her hands. She wanted to touch him, hold him, but... "I don't want to hurt you."

"Then stop crying, Chloe." He held out his hand at kind of an awkward angle, she supposed because that was the only way he could manage it. She took his hand, and he squeezed.

Him, lying in a hospital bed, trying to make *her* feel better. She grabbed the chair that was situated a ways away from the bed and drew it closer so she could sit next to him. So she could press her forehead to his hand. She couldn't quite stop crying, but she tried.

"I'm not sure I would have... I'm glad you're okay. I'm..." She looked up. Met his gaze. Pain was in his expression. Physical. Emotional. The whole gamut. "How about we leave it at, I love you and I'm glad you're here."

He smiled a little, but he didn't say anything at first. Just kept looking at her in a way that made her want to fidget.

"What do you say we get married?"

Her mouth dropped open because *what*? "What?"

"We've been together for about a year now. Why not?"

"Because a million reasons. And we have *not* been together. Sneaking around to have sex is *not* being together. What kind of meds are you on?"

"Okay." He yawned, winced a little. "We can wait."

She didn't know why that made her feel deflated. She clearly just needed sleep. But he just lay there in the bed, holding her hand, starting to look sleepy and...

"I put in an application to Bent County." She hadn't been going to tell him. Not until she got the job—*if* she got the job. But it just seemed right, somehow.

It was his turn to be surprised. "What?"

"They're starting a K-9 unit, and I wanted to be a part of it."

"I thought the applications on that closed a few months back?"

"They did, but one of the people fell through, so they've got one position. I… I didn't do it originally because I didn't want anyone to think I was doing it for you. To have you." She swallowed, looked down at their entwined hands. "I didn't want *you* to think that, or maybe I was afraid that… I don't know. Afraid. Period. Always. I just… The past few days have been a mess, but it was a mess you were there through. No matter what. You didn't leave my side. Even when it hurt. Even when it got you shot. You were there and…"

She looked up at him.

"Chloe, marry me. Please. Because no matter what, I'm always going to be there."

She wanted to laugh. And cry. And…agree. Most of all, agree. Not try to think it through, not try to worry it out. She just wanted him. "Okay," she managed.

"What changed your mind?"

"Seemed wrong to say no twice to a guy who was shot twice by my own mother," she said, sniffling as tears kept falling over her cheeks.

"Yeah, that is a bit much."

But it wasn't the truth. There were so many truths, but the main one had hit her over the head when she'd first come in. "You look at me the way Walker looks at Mary."

"I believe that's called *lovesick*."

"I'll take it. Because I've never had… No one's ever cared. Not the way you do. And you're not perfect. I want to punch you half the time, but you are the best man I know, Jack Hudson."

"That's mighty handy, because I happen to believe you deserve some best, Chloe Brink. And I plan on giving it to you."

And Jack Hudson always came through on plans.

* * * * *